FIONA OF THE GLEN

CATRIONA GUNN

Copyright (C) 2021 Catriona Gunn

Layout design and Copyright (C) 2021 by Next Chapter

Published 2021 by Next Chapter

Edited by Megan Gaudino

Cover art by CoverMint

This book is a work of fiction. Names, characters, places, and incidents are the product of the author's imagination or are used fictitiously. Any resemblance to actual events, locales, or persons, living or dead, is purely coincidental.

All rights reserved. No part of this book may be reproduced or transmitted in any form or by any means, electronic or mechanical, including photocopying, recording, or by any information storage and retrieval system, without the author's permission.

This book is dedicated to all those Highland women, men, and children who suffered from the Clearances and their descendants, wherever they now live.

CLAN GUNN

PRELUDE

It has long been a legend in our family that the females wrote about events leading to their marriage. Gunn family folklore claimed that the records stretched back for centuries, transcribed in leather-bound volumes securely locked in a brass-bound trunk. Nobody knows who started the tradition, but the eldest Gunn daughter was the guardian of the records wherever she happened to be.

In Scotland, of course, it has always been legal for married women to retain their maiden names if they so wished. That fact makes it easier to trace our family line from generation to generation.

When the Second World War erupted in 1939, the army requisitioned the house where the trunk resided, and the records disappeared. The legend continued, but with the disappearance of centuries of history, the tradition withered and died. For a couple of generations, the practice was remembered rather than followed.

Then, in early 2017, government cutbacks shrunk the army. The government put the old Gunn property on the market. The contents were put to public auction in a saleroom in Edinburgh's George Street, and as fate would have it, a distant cousin of ours bought the trunk. As soon as she realised what was inside, our cousin contacted the family. I was present as we gathered in Edinburgh and sifted through the contents. We found over twenty volumes, stretching back for hundreds of years. Some authors had used beautiful copperplate writing, others only contrived a nearly illegible scrawl, with stains that could come from tears, wine, or even blood. At least one writer had used mediaeval Gaelic, and others we have not yet opened.

After a long family conference that included every female member of our branch of the Gunn's, and many interested males, we decided to consider these journals historical documents. Some of us wondered if we should send the volumes to a museum or a library. After a heated debate, we decided not to, as we believed the curators would consign the memoirs to some archives where nobody would read them.

Instead, we thought that we would transcribe these stories for the interest of the general public and any Gunn family historian. Once we arrived at that decision, there was the question of finding an understanding publisher that would consider such a diverse range of material. If we were lucky, the publisher might think the memoirs possessed sufficient literary merit to bring into the public domain.

Fortunately, I discovered a publisher who bravely agreed to take a chance with this eclectic collection, if only one at a time. I took on the task of transcribing the volumes, which, in some cases, needed very little amendment and in others required a considerable re-write to ensure they were more suitable for modern tastes.

I hope that this first volume interests and entertains the readers as much as it does me.

Catriona Gunn

I

Glen nan Gall, Scottish Highlands, Summer, 1823.

I was sitting on the wall when the soldiers marched into the glen. I was not sure why they came but immediately knew that they would be trouble.

"Father," I called out, "the redcoats are coming."

Father joined me, leaning against the unmortared stone as he puffed on his pipe and watched the long column of scarlet thread along the track.

"They'll be heading to the old castle," he said.

"How do you know that?" I asked.

"There is nowhere else for them to go on this road," Father said, breathing out smoke that was foul enough to keep the midges at bay.

"They could go over the pass," I said, trying to prove my local knowledge.

"It's late afternoon," Father said and glanced upward. "And there is rain coming. The pass is fifteen miles long. They will halt at the old castle."

The soldiers were making good time along the track with two tall officers in the lead and hectoring sergeants on either flank. I could see the last of the sun gleaming on the gold braid on the officers' uniforms and the great white stripes on the sergeants' arms.

"You stay here," Father instructed. "Count them as they pass and find out what regiment they are."

"How do I do that?" I asked.

"Ask them," Father spoke over his shoulder as he strode away. "Remember that they'll be English speakers. They won't have the Gaelic."

"I have the English," I said.

"Then use that tongue. " Father's words came to me from a long distance away.

When I looked for him, he had vanished. Father could do that. One minute he was tall and broad and as bold as Fingal, the next he had disappeared among the heather.

I counted forty soldiers, some quite middle-aged men but most very young, mere boys who looked uncomfortable in their ill-fitting scarlet that matched the colour of their faces. Mud spattered their boots and black trousers while the sergeants barely took a breath between insults and swearwords. I decided that I did not like these sergeants very much at all.

"Halloa!" I called out, shifting my stance, so I perched on the soldiers' side of the wall and swinging my legs from side to side. It was quite pleasant sitting on the warm stone with my bare feet cool. "Where are you going?"

The taller of the two officers glanced at me and looked away without a word. His companion was younger, with less gold on his tunic and a more open face.

He grinned at me. "We're going to Dunbeiste".

I had to struggle to understand his pronunciation of our castle. "Why go to Dunbeiste?" I asked artlessly. "There is nothing there."

"Not yet!" The younger officer stepped aside as his colleagues marched past with their shakos tall on their heads and their muskets held upright, barrels dark in the sunlight. "We are going to garrison it," he told me. He was a very open man, with sandy hair and freckles that merged when he smiled. I would have rather liked him had he not been a soldier.

"Why on earth would you do that?" I asked, widening my eyes in the manner that always worked with the boys in the glen. It was just as effective with this young officer; I was glad to see.

"Oh, we're here to stop the smugglers," my gallant lad said, as open as you please.

I looked around as if I had no idea what he meant. "Smugglers?" I said. "You mean all those French luggers carrying brandy and silks?" I shook my head, allowing my hair to shiver around my face. "We're miles from the sea here, Captain."

"I'm only an Ensign, actually," my officer said. "Ensign Andrew Hepburn, Ma'am, at your service." He gave the most refined of little bows and rose again with his shako lopsided on his head and a grin on his face.

"I am Fiona Gunn," I said.

"Pleased to make your acquaintance, Miss Gunn," Ensign Hepburn said. "We're stopping the whisky smuggling," he told me and lowered his voice. "I believe this entire area is rife with whisky smugglers."

"Oh," I whispered and looked around as if expecting to see the infernal rogues leaping from every shrub of heather. "Are you sure you have come to the right glen?"

"I do hope so," Ensign Hepburn said, with every appearance of alarm on his face. "This is Glen nan Gall isn't it?"

"That's correct. Glen nan Gall, the Glen of Strangers." I nodded.

"What a strange name," Ensign Hepburn said. "Why is it called that?"

"It's an old name," I told him. "This glen is where all the broken men and the unwanted came, from the ancient Picts to the Jacobites. Why," I said, "Have you never heard the legend of

Naked Iain? He was the sole survivor of the Battle of Cromdale, and he staggered into the glen without a stitch on and became part of us."

"I do not know that," Ensign Hepburn said.

"He was the reason the glen did not rise for the Jacobites," I told him. "We did not fight for King George either. We are our own people and not inclined to follow any king or chief."

Let him make what he wishes from that, I thought.

"Mr. Hepburn!" The bellow came from the taller officer. "Stop dawdling!"

"I think your colonel wants you," I said. "Maybe you had better run along."

"Oh, he's not a colonel," Hepburn said, adjusting his shako, which seemed set to fall entirely off his head.

"That's Captain Barrow."

"Oh," I said. "Of the Sutherland Fencibles, I believe?"

"Indeed not," Ensign Hepburn said. "Whatever gave you that idea? We are the South Edinburgh Militia."

"That's what I meant," I said, smiling as my bold ensign gave another bow and then ran off after the column.

I watched his legs twinkle in the tight white breeches that looked painfully uncomfortable and waited for Father to reappear.

"Well?" Father said as he emerged from the heather.

"Forty men of the South Edinburgh Militia," I reported at once. "Captain Barrow leads them, Ensign Hepburn is second in command, and they are here to suppress the whisky smuggling. The men are a mixture of recruits and old hands, while the sergeants are martinets. They will base themselves in Dunbeiste."

Father patted my arm. "Well done, Fiona. We don't need spies when you're around. We'll have to make their life a mite uncomfortable." His grin was as evil as I had ever seen. "So that was Captain Barrow of the South Edinburgh Militia, eh? We'll see how long the good captain and his tin soldiers last when winter bites the glen."

"Father," I said. "Be careful."

"Oh, I will." He rubbed a peat-stained hand across his jaw. "We're taking a consignment down to Perth at the end of the week. We'll see how good our Captain Barrow is then."

I slipped off the wall and brushed the moss from the back of my skirt.

"And where are you going?" Father asked.

"I'm going to watch the soldiers," I said. "Mother does not need me just now, and I want to see what they're doing." I smoothed my hand down my gown and said nothing about my freckle-faced young officer. I hoped that Father did not guess.

"You're playing with fire there," he said, knowing at once what I was up to, the cunning old fox. "Best avoid the sojer-lads. There are decent men enough in the glen without having to go further afield."

"Yes, Father." I pretended meekness even as I thought of his freckles and the tight breeches. "I am only going to look."

Father sighed; he knew the hot blood of the Gunns. After all, he had been married to my mother for upwards of twenty-one years and sired a brood of children.

"Don't do anything stupid now, Fiona."

He knew me well enough not to say more. Canute had more chance of controlling the tide than any man had of preventing a Gunn woman from doing something on which she had set her mind.

"I won't."

Dunbeiste was only a couple of miles up the glen, a gaunt grey shell of a place with a grim history. Lifting my skirt above the rough grass in the centre of the track, I followed the Militia, listening to the regular thump of their boots on the ground and wondering what they thought about our glen. They must have felt very far from home, these men from South Edinburgh, away down in the Low Country.

They were arriving at the castle when I caught up with them, so I found a perch on Creag Thairbh— the Bulls Rock— tucked my skirt underneath me, and settled down to watch.

Captain Barrow stood apart from the others, giving crisp orders that my Ensign Hepburn hurried to obey. I noted that the sergeants' job seemed to consist of shouting at, pushing, and occasionally striking the poor soldier-men, for whom I almost felt sorry.

After an hour, a wagon lurched along the track, nearly spilling its load as its wheels sunk into the mud. It came to a halt outside the walls of the castle.

In an instant, there was increased pandemonium as Captain Barrow screamed orders that sent the poor little militiamen running to the wagon to unload what turned out to be tents and blankets, food of some kind, and other necessities. It was fascinating to see the soldier boys at work, setting up three neat lines of tents outside the stone walls and even raising a flag pole.

Every so often, a face turned toward me as one soldier or another wondered who I was and why I was there, but I did not respond or wave. I had my reasons for observing and was quite happy to watch.

Late summer evenings were long in our glen, and it was late before there was insufficient light for the men to work.

I saw the clouds of midges rise from the heather in the gloaming and smiled at the antics of the lowlanders. Perhaps they believed that flapping their hands would chase away the swarms. Maybe they believed that the presence of two score redcoats could end distilling in the glen. Perhaps they believed that the moon was made of sour milk and dragons ate grass.

The flash from the slopes of Am Bodach attracted my attention then, two high hills dominate the head, Am Bodach, the Old Man, and An Cailleach, the Old Woman. When the path leaves Dunbeiste, it winds up Bealach nan Bo, the Pass of the Cattle, which crept between these twin mountains and south to Perthshire.

I saw the brief light from the corner of my eye and did not move. Such a flash could only come from the sun reflecting on something, water, metal, or glass, and I knew that section of the hill had no water. Metal or glass indicated a human presence—somebody was up there. The glen was certainly busy today, what with this stranger up Am Bodach and the soldiers scurrying about Dunbeiste.

Whatever I thought about soldiers then, there was no mistaking the beauty of the trumpet call that sent them to bed. Last Post must be one of the most soul-stirring sounds in creation and to hear it played against a Highland sunset is something that everybody should experience at least once in their life. Indeed, it may have been the melancholic beauty of that sound, combined with the lowering of the colourful Union flag, that enticed me to linger longer than I had intended.

I was still sitting on Creag Thairbh when Ensign Hepburn left the pretty little camp and walked up the hillside. He was not aware of my presence until I spoke.

"Good evening, Ensign Hepburn."

The poor boy nearly leapt a yard into the air.

"Oh, my goodness. Miss Gunn. I did not see you there."

"It's the dark," I told him solemnly. "It hides things. And people." He looked even younger in the fading evening light.

"I just came up here for a smoke." The ensign produced a long-stemmed pipe.

I was unsure if he was asking my permission or proving his manhood by allowing himself such an adult occupation.

"I see." I watched as he stuffed tobacco into the bowl of his pipe and scraped a spark from his tinder-box. "Do you like our castle?"

"It's a very stark castle," Ensign Hepburn said.

"It is all of that," I agreed.

"It has a very unusual name, Dunbeiste. Does that mean anything?" Ensign Hepburn blew smoke into the air, which seemed to encourage the midges that clouded around his head.

I smiled. "A dun is a fort or castle, and beiste is a monster, so it means the fort of the monster." I waited for his comments.

"The fort of the monster? Pray, tell me, Miss Gunn, what sort of monster lives in this fort? Is it a dragon?"

That was strange that he should think of a dragon so soon after I had done the same. I began to like this freckled officer.

"No," I said. "The monster was one of the previous owners. He was a man named Comyn, and he used to make the young women work naked in the fields at harvest time."

Ensign Hepburn nearly choked on his pipe, which was amusing. I patted his back to help him breathe again.

"That must have been quite a sight," he eventually said.

"I imagine so." I waited until he was about to draw on his pipe again before I spoke, "They killed him," I said and looked away when he spluttered again.

"Who killed him?" Ensign Hepburn asked.

"The girls' mothers killed him," I said. "One was a witch, and she called on the eagles. When Comyn was riding back to the glen, an eagle swooped on him and frightened his horse. He fell and broke his leg." I waited for a few moments as the sun sunk behind the western rampart of hills and the sky finally darkened. "It was three days before a traveller found his body, torn to pieces by eagles, or something much worse."

Ensign Hepburn did not look quite so gallant now. He was a long way from home in this Highland glen. "What could be worse?"

I screwed up my face as if I had not anticipated the question. "The hills have their secrets," I said, trying to sound mysterious. "It may be Comyn that haunts the castle or someone else. The builders placed a human sacrifice in the foundations, you see."

"Oh," Ensign Hepburn said. "Are there other stories in this glen?"

"Everything has a story," I slapped the boulder on which I sat. "This rock is Creag Thairbh, the bull's rock, where the old folk used to sacrifice bulls in the long-gone days. And out there —" I nodded into the dark— "there is Clach-nan-chat."

"What does that mean?" my captive audience asked.

"It means the Rock of the Cat because the wildcat nests there." I was quite prepared to continue, for there were stories in every corner of Glen nan Beiste.

"Oh," Ensign Hepburn took a final puff of his pipe. "I'd better get back to the camp," he said. "In case there are whisky smugglers, you understand. I have my duty to do."

"Of course, you must do your duty," I said. "Well, sleep tight, Ensign Hepburn, and don't think about the ghosts and bogles." I touched his arm, fully aware that he would think of little except ghosts now, and walked away, deliberately swaying my hips to unsettle this raw militiaman even further. It was only fair that I should give him something to watch after I had admired his tight breeches.

I smiled; Father would be proud of me for doing my part in making these redcoats unhappy. Glen nan Gall was ours and not a place for South Countrymen to infest with their alien ways.

As I left Creag Thairbh, I heard movement high on Am Bodach. It was nearly full dark by then and sound travels far in the night hours. Glen-born and bred, I'm aware of all the usual night sounds, from the lowing of cattle to the rustle of a mouse under the heather, the shriek of a hunting owl, and the grunting of autumn deer. This sound was none of these. It was the thump of a boot on heather. A man was walking down Am Bodach, and he was not of the South Edinburgh Militia.

2

Father turned his head from side to side to examine the heather pegs he was making.

"There could be a hundred reasons for a man on the hillside," he said. "I'll pass the word around and see if it was any one of us. If not, then I will worry."

I said nothing. I had told Father and now I would forget all about the stranger on the hill. It was no longer my concern. Other things, however, were.

"He was a handsome enough boy," Mother looked up from the spinning wheel she had moved outside to get the benefit of the sunlight. "Does he interest you?"

I thought about Ensign Hepburn with his clipped, Edinburgh accent and his freckled face. I could not help smiling. "He is very shy," I said, "and he has slender hands."

"He has slender hands?" Mother repeated. "Is that a good point or a bad point?"

By that time, our conversation had attracted a clutch of my siblings, so five shining-haired children aged from fifteen to five were listening intently.

"Well, Fiona," Dougal said with all the subtlety of a ten-year-old. "What do slender hands have to do with it?"

"I can't see him digging peat with small white hands," I said. "Or bringing in the harvest."

Mother smiled. "Not everybody lives like us. Slender hands may be an asset in South Edinburgh."

"I don't want to live in South Edinburgh," I said. "And anyway, Ensign Hepburn's first name is Andrew."

"What's wrong with the name Andrew?" Mother sounded confused. "Andrew is an excellent name."

"I don't want a man called Andrew," I said. "I want a man called Murdoch."

Mother shook her head. "What am I going to do with you, Fiona? I honestly don't know."

Father smiled. "You seemed comfortable in Andrew's company when I saw you. Now, tomorrow is the last day of the term," he said. "You know what that means, don't you?"

"Yes, it means we have to pay our rent."

"It means that you have to get over to the Factor's house and pay before he comes to the door. The last thing we need is that nosey bug—" Father stopped there. He had been about to swear, but stopped. Father believed that I was too young to hear such words. "The last thing we need is that inquisitive fellow poking around the glen."

"Yes, father." I was tempted to say, "he is a nosey bugger," but I decided not to upset my father. Not out of any feelings of respect and certainly not from fear, but because he was a decent old stick, and did his best.

"Come." Father crooked his finger, and I followed him into the house.

Our home was typical of the Highland homes of the period. We called them black houses and I believe that name is still in use, although there are far fewer such buildings around now, with the Clearances and so-called Improvements. From the outside, they looked like a pile of loose stones, with unmortared rubble-build topped by heather thatch. Sometimes the heather made a black house appear like part of the surroundings, nearly hiding it. The windows were small and deep-set into the thick walls, and we had a barrel set into the roof to guide out the smoke. There were definite advantages to such a building, with the heather and thick walls keeping out all the coarse weather, while inside it was warm in winter and cool in summer.

"Right now, Fiona. Step with me."

I followed Father inside.

Mother came with us and busied herself with a broom, brushing the stone flags and shouting at some of my brothers and sisters.

"Where are you going, Calum?" Mother asked.

"Tomorrow is Quarter Day," Father said and pointed to the hearthstone.

"Don't you go making a mess, now," Mother warned.

"I wouldn't dare," Father said, quite truthfully, I thought.

Even in summer, the fire in the centre of the living room burned brightly. Father took a square, flat stone from its position against the wall and carefully slid it under the piled-up peats, using a shovel to keep each burning cube where it belonged. With Mother watching critically, he placed the fire slightly to the side and levered up the hearthstone before delving into the hollow beneath.

"My secret treasure store," he told me as if I had not seen it every Quarter Day for the past twenty years.

Hauling out an oblong metal box about twelve inches long, he levered off the lid and emptied the contents onto the oak table that was Mother's pride and joy. A cascade of silver and copper coins poured onto the table, brightened with a single gold sovereign.

I looked in awe at this fabulous display of wealth, as I did every Quarter Day.

"Here." Father carefully counted out some coins and passed them to Mother, who folded them into a linen handkerchief and tucked it into the pocket of my skirt.

"You take care of that, now." Mother said. "You know what to do."

"Yes, Mother," I assured her.

As the oldest of her children, I was responsible for paying the rent to the Factor. Father refused to have anything to do with the man and, for some reason, also ensured that Mother would not go. I did not mind. It got me out of the glen four times every year and allowed me to see a different set of faces.

"Off you go, then," Mother gave me a pat on the bottom, as she always did.

I walked across the glen and over the Bealach Garbh, the Rough Pass, out to the north. It is sufficient to say that I arrived in the small town of Charlestown of Aberlour, where the Factor had his office and looked around with delight.

Perhaps city girls were used to shops and large buildings, even stage coaches and other conveniences, but to a girl from the glens, even the small town was a bit overwhelming. I am a Gunn, though, so I adopted a confident swagger and looked for the Factor's office.

There were a few more houses since I had been here last, with shops with shiny glass windows and signs above the doors. I struggled to read the English words in some and found that the Factor had moved. His name was in gold letters against a green background. *Charles Snodgrass: Solicitor and Estate Manager*

If I had hesitated before such an intimidating place, I might have lost my nerve, so I pushed straight in. There was a polished wooden counter with a brass bell that I lifted and rang as if my life depended on it.

"All right! I'm coming!" Charles Snodgrass appeared tall and handsome and about the same age as my parents, yet he could have come from a different world. Where my father was dark-haired and nut-brown from spending most of his life outside, Charles Snodgrass was smooth-skinned and blonde-haired. While Father dressed in rough homespun clothing or even in a kilt, Charles Snodgrass wore an immaculate dove grey suit with a fancy waistcoat with mother-of-pearl buttons. While Father spoke Gaelic as a first language and only lapsed into English when forced, Charles Snodgrass greeted me in English.

"Good afternoon," he said. His eyes roved from the top of my hatless head to the mud on my bare feet and back. I was never sure that I liked the expression that came into Mr Snodgrass's eyes on these occasions.

"Good afternoon," I said politely. "I have come to pay the rent. My father is Calum Gunn of Glen nan Gall."

"Oh." Mr Snodgrass's expression altered to an insincere smile. "You are Mrs Gunn's daughter."

"I am." I agreed. "Could I pay the rent, please? And Mother says I am to get a receipt or I have not to part with a brass farthing."

Mr Snodgrass nearly smiled. "Come through the back," he invited, as he always did.

I padded through, with the floorboards cool under my feet.

The back shop was stuffy, with two tall oil lamps pooling yellow light onto a roll-top desk, piled with ledgers and files. There were two seats, one of dark red leather. which Mr Snodgrass settled himself into, and the other, of plain wood, which I occupied without asking his permission. I may have been a girl from the glens, but I knew sufficient about good manners to know that a gentleman should not sit before a lady. Mr Snodgrass then was no gentleman, and therefore I had no requirements to act like a lady.

Mr Snodgrass eyed me up and down with that same leer in his eyes. I did not like him.

"I have brought the rent," I reminded, wishing to finish in that room as quickly as possible.

Mr Snodgrass leaned across the desk as I emptied the rent money. He counted the coins carefully, and the back of his hand would have brushed against my breast had I not pulled back as far as the chair would allow.

"Well, now, Fiona." Mr Snodgrass's smile was unpleasant. "I

am afraid that you are short of a shilling or two. I am sure that we can come to some other arrangement to ensure that your family is not evicted."

I felt the colour rush to my cheeks. "The money is right," I said, knowing that my father's arithmetic was immaculate.

"Oh, perhaps it was correct for last quarter. Did you not know that the new owner has put up the rents? You are five shillings short." Mr Snodgrass shook his head. "It is such a shame, but I'm sure that you and I can come to a suitable arrangement to make up the shortfall." His wink was as amiable as one of the Nile crocodiles that the minister mentioned to frighten his congregation.

I felt the colour rise to my cheeks. I could guess what type of suitable arrangement Mr Snodgrass had in mind, and it was not one to which I was prepared to agree.

"Shop!" The deep roar came as a great relief. I had not heard the outer door open. "Is there anybody at home?"

Mr Snodgrass looked up. "I won't be a minute," he said. "Think about what I said. It would be good for any tenant family to have me as their friend, Fiona. There could be a rent reduction, and as your mother now has eight mouths to feed, every penny is necessary." He stood up, rubbing his hand down my arm as he passed me.

I took a deep breath and wondered if I could run out the door. I knew I could not. Mother had said I was to pay the rent and get a receipt, so I would do that. I heard the murmur of voices through the door that separated the back room from the front office. After a few minutes, I grew bored and opened the door a crack to see what was happening.

Mr Snodgrass sat with his back to me, facing a tall, weatherbeaten man across the width of the counter.

"Are you sure you know what you're doing?" Charles Snodgrass poised his quill above the bottom of the document.

"I'm sure." The other man spoke with an accent I had never heard before, a long drawl that was very pleasant on the ear.

"Indeed,'" Mr Snodgrass said. Diving under the counter, he produced a small sheaf of papers, neatly tied in a linen tape. "Here we are then, Mr Gillespie." Clearing a space on the surface of the desk, he carefully untied the tape and unfolded the top document. "You know the asking price?"

"I am aware of the asking price, Mr Snodgrass." Gillespie put forward his hand for the documents, but Snodgrass pulled them closer.

"I cannot allow you to view these, Mr Gillespie—" there was suspicion on his face as Snodgrass looked up from behind the desk— "until I have proof that you can obtain the money." Scottish solicitors were not known for their cordial reception, especially on a Monday morning, and Gillespie, with his weather-worn face and outdoors clothing, did not belong in Snodgrass's comfortable environment.

"You'll have all the proof you want," Gillespie promised, "when I know what I'm buying." Ignoring Snodgrass's protests, he reached across the desk and dragged the papers toward him. "The entire glen, I see, from Bealach nan Bo to the summit of Am Bodach and Bealach Garbh to An Cailleach and the watershed of the feeder burns." He looked up. "Does this include mineral and water rights, pasturage, and the tenancies?"

Snodgrass sighed as if talking to a man of limited intelligence. "Of course it does. The entire glen and watershed of the Allt Gobhlach—" he stumbled over the Gaelic words— "and all attendant rights are included in the purchase price." His pause was significant, as was the contemptuous curl of his thin lips. "But only to a purchaser with enough funds." He looked Gillespie up and down, expertly calculating the cost of his clothes and the value of the battered metal watch chain that crossed his waistcoat.

"Why is it for sale so soon?" Gillespie asked the question quietly, but his eyes were sharp as he waited for the answer.

"So soon?" Snodgrass temporised.

"You handled the sale of the glen just last year," Gillespie reminded gently. "And a year previous to that."

Snodgrass shrugged. "There are many reasons for selling land."

"So I believe," Gillespie said quietly. "Could you tell me the reason for selling Glen nan Gall?"

The atmosphere in the room tightened until it was brittle.

Snodgrass removed his spectacles and began to polish the lenses. "Mr—ah— Gillespie. I am duty-bound not to divulge my client's reason for disposing of his property. That is a confidential matter." He slid quietly behind the legal terminology of his trade.

"You are temporising, Mr Snodgrass," Gillespie said quietly.

A moment ago, he had been the object of suspicion, but now he was a predator, an intruder into this place of ledgers and documents, legal tomes and word-splitting debate.

Gillespie leaned across the desk, holding Snodgrass's eyes. I slid slightly back in case he saw me looking. This Mr Gillespie was an interesting man, with a long, lean face and hair that was too unkempt to be fashionable.

"If I'm to purchase this property, I surely have the right to know its faults."

"Glen nan Gall has all the potential of any Highland estate." Surprisingly, Snodgrass did not back down. "If it was improved, the purchaser could use the land for agricultural or sporting purposes."

"If it was improved," Gillespie repeated the words slowly. "Do you know what *improved* means, Mr Snodgrass?"

When Snodgrass replied, it was evident that he chose his words carefully. "What landowners do with their property is entirely their own affair, Mr Gillespie. I dare say that you would affect improvements, of whatever sort, to Glen nan Gall if you were to find the purchase price." He raised his eyebrows in mocking expectation.

"Remind me," Gillespie said. "What was the asking price again?"

Snodgrass whispered a figure that I could not hear, and Gillespie nodded.

"I'll give you that."

"I need proof that you have the means," Snodgrass insisted.

"In cash," Gillespie said.

"In cash?" Snodgrass looked more interested than he had a moment before.

Reaching into his leather portmanteau, Gillespie produced four small bags. Each one dropped on the desk with a cheerful *chink*.

"In gold," Gillespie said.

I nearly fell off my chair in astonishment. I had seen perhaps three gold sovereigns in my life and believed that Father's secret hoard under the hearthstone was the height of wealth. Now, this Mr Gillespie with the strange drawling accent had produced four bags that he claimed were stuffed with gold.

"Is that all gold?" Snodgrass seemed as surprised as I was. His eyes fixed on the bags, but he kept his hands firmly on his side of the desk.

In answer, Gillespie opened the first bag and cascaded the contents onto the table. Golden guineas and golden sovereigns rattled and bounced from the meagre space between the ledgers, slithering onto the stained wooden floor and dropping on to the floor to roll around Snodgrass's spindly ankles.

Gasping, the solicitor pulled his chair slightly further back, allowing the coins to settle in front of him.

"All gold," Gillespie confirmed. "And all four bags are the same." As Snodgrass reached forward, Gillespie clamped down his hand on the solicitor's wrist. "Paperwork first, then payment."

"It will take some time," Snodgrass stared at the pyramid of gold that decorated his desk. The cynicism had altered to greed.

"We have all day and all night," Gillespie assured him. "And all tomorrow, if need be."

Well, I had not such a generous allocation of time. I had to get back to the glen to check on the cattle and do whatever chores Mother had found for me. These men, with their business deals, have no consideration for the work women have to do. Bags of gold might be all very impressive, but farms don't run themselves.

Scooping up the unopened bags, Gillespie replaced them inside his portmanteau before returning the loose coins from the desk back into their bag.

"I'll leave those on the floor for you to collect," Gillespie said. "Once you have finished with the legal niceties." Withdrawing a couple of steps, he sat on the hard-backed chair in the corner of the room. "I can wait." Pulling a long cheroot from inside his pocket, he lit it at the flame of the candle and sat back. He picked up his broad-brimmed hat from the floor, slanted it over his forehead and watched Snodgrass from narrowed eyes.

For a long moment, Snodgrass looked as if he were going to ask Gillespie to put out his cheroot, but then he sighed, lifted his quill and began to write.

After a while, he looked up, his Presbyterian conscience obviously at odds with his legal duty. "You may be purchasing trouble, you know."

Gillespie nodded. "There will be trouble," he said.

When Gillespie looked up, Snodgrass stared directly into his eyes and shivered. He returned to his labours, and the scratching of the quill was the only sound in that room.

I sat in increasing impatience, well aware that my small amount of money did not matter to Snodgrass compared to Mr Gillespie's impressive financial transaction. All the same, it would've been good to be remembered.

"Very well, Mr Gillespie." Snodgrass eventually pressed the end of his quill down and wrote his name. I could see that the elegant letters were steady on the paper. He finished with a flourish. "That's my part of the deed done," he said. "Now, all you have to do is sign your name beside the cross, and you become the legal owner." He passed the document across the desk and leaned back in his chair. "Make sure you understand every detail, Mr Gillespie. If you have any doubts, ask me."

Mr Gillespie took hold of the document and scrutinised it. He seemed to check every word for mistakes, checked the accompanying map, and then finally lifted the quill from its position beside the inkwell.

I had not noticed the grandfather clock in the corner of the room, but now it gave its loud tick as the pendulum swung away the seconds. I glanced at the time, it was nearly nine o'clock in the evening and darkness was falling outside. Rain smeared the small panes of glass in the window that reflected the flame of the tall candle.

I saw Mr Gillespie poise the quill above the faintly pencilled cross; he seemed to be lost in thought for a long minute, and then he flexed his wrist and added his name to the document. He wrote so firmly that the point of the quill broke, and darkblue ink spilt in a blot that spread across the page. I wondered if that would spoil the meaning of the paper but apparently it did not.

Snodgrass stepped forward and pressed blotting paper onto the mess with a deft hand. "And here, please?" He proffered a copy of another document. Rather than sign immediately, Mr Gillespie read the papers with every bit as much care as he had with the original before he lifted a fresh quill, dipped it in the inkwell and added his signature.

"That appears to be that, Mr Gillespie."

I was unsure if there was satisfaction or relief in his voice as Snodgrass checked both signatures before filing one copy of the deed and sliding the other across the top of his desk to Mr Gillespie.

"You might find the inhabitants of the glen a little…reticent,"

Snodgrass said slowly. "Despite the name, they have a reputation of being less than friendly to those they don't know. However, I am sure you took that into account."

Mr Gillespie said nothing, and I looked at this man who had purchased our glen. I opened the door further to ensure that I heard, proud to think how I would relate this tale when I returned home. To my astonishment, I overbalanced and toppled into the door, which opened, propelling me face down into the front room in a flurry of skirts, arms and bare legs.

"Good God!" Mr Snodgrass stepped back as quickly as Mr Gillespie stepped forward. I felt Gillespie's strong hands on me as he helped me to my feet.

"Are you all right, young lady? That was quite a tumble you took."

"I am all right." I was only hurt in my pride and quickly apologised for interrupting their meeting. "I was just paying our rent," I said, gabbling to cover my embarrassment and with my face as red as an autumn dawn.

"I see." Mr Gillespie was not as old as I would have expected for a landowner. He could not have been much past thirty, with the brightest eyes that I had ever seen. "Well then, Miss, I suggest that you complete your business and get on your way."

I glanced at Mr Snodgrass. "I've to get a receipt," I said, "but Mr Snodgrass told me that the new landowner had put up the rent, and we are five shillings short so we may get evicted." I waited for a moment to see if Mr Gillespie reacted. "Mr Snodgrass said that he and I could come to some other agreement for the shortfall—" I had not finished my sentence before Mr Snodgrass interrupted.

"I am sure we can allow a week's grace."

"Where is it you live?" Mr Gillespie asked. "As a very recent landowner myself– as I am sure you heard– I can guess how important the rents are to the estate."

He had guessed that I had been listening. I coloured again. "I live in Glen nan Gall," I said.

Mr Gillespie raised his eyebrows. "And the new landowner put up the rent, did he? As the even newer landowner, I can say that they are now back down to the old level. Pray give this young lady her receipt, Mr Snodgrass and allow her to be on her way."

I waited, trembling slightly, as Mr Snodgrass hurriedly wrote a receipt and handed it to me with all the good grace that he could muster.

"Thank you," I said and then tried to leave the office. I could feel Snodgrass's discomfiture and knew that he would seek revenge on me for thus exposing him. The people of Glen nan Gall did not care for our Factor.

"Are you going home tonight?" Mr Gillespie asked.

"Yes, sir," I said, and after a few moments, added. "Thank you." I doubted whether Mr Gillespie knew why I was thanking him, and it was not only for the five-shilling reduction in rent.

"I have a carriage outside," Mr Gillespie said. "I am going part of the way."

"No, sir," I said in a perfect panic.

I may have been only a girl from the glens with no knowledge of life, but I knew enough never to step inside a carriage with a strange man. However kind Mr Gillespie had appeared with his rapid rent reduction, he might've been an entirely different man when alone with me in the privacy of his carriage.

I shook my head with far more violence than I had intended and fled from that room, not forgetting to thank him again for his kindness on my way out the door.

3

My father was not happy when I told him about Mr Snodgrass's behaviour. I saw him draw himself up and reach to the thatch above, where he stored his pistols.

"No, Calum. Mother placed a hand on his arm. "That is not the answer."

"I'll kill him." Father was never known for his tact and diplomacy.

"Maybe later," Mother said. "But next quarter, Calum, you and I will go to pay the rent together. Fiona will remain here."

Father grunted and withdrew his hand from the thatch as Mother looked at me with something like relief.

"Of course, Fiona may have different plans for the future. You are twenty years old now, Fiona. It's high time you found yourself a nice young man and settled down." Her smile was as cunning as any Highland fox. "Have you thought more about that young ensign with the slender hands?"

"I have not thought about him at all," I lied. I had enlivened my journey back across the Bealach Garbh with memories of Ensign Hepburn's freckled face and tight breeches. I was as red-blooded as any Gunn woman.

"There is a ceilidh tonight," Father reminded me. "Mother and I will be attending." He looked at Mother meaningfully.

"You are not going for the music, Calum," Mother said.

"I have my reasons," Father said.

"Remember there are soldiers in Dunbeiste now," Mother warned, "and a new landowner about whom we know nothing. Don't be taking any foolish risks. You are no longer a youngster of twenty."

"There won't be any risks," Father was visibly annoyed to be reminded of his advancing years. He must have been all of forty-two.

"And don't go hurting anybody either," Mother continued.

"I thought we were talking about Fiona finding a man, not me making some money." Father turned the conversation back to me and smiled at the dirty look I threw at him.

"We are," Mother said. "Niall Grant will be at the ceilidh. He is a decent lad."

"Niall is all right," I agreed hesitantly. I knew all about Niall Grant and his ways.

"Good." Mother sat back with a look of satisfaction on her face. "You can talk to him tomorrow. He's a good looking sort of lad and hard working. He won't let you down, and his hands are not slender, even though his name is not Murdoch."

I said nothing to that, despite knowing more about Niall Grant than Mother realised. I gave a small smile that I hoped disguised my feelings. I also wondered if Ensign Hepburn would venture out of his cold castle to join the fun.

"As long as that stranger does not come in." Father's words curiously echoed some of my thoughts.

"Oh, he's all right," I said, thinking of Ensign Hepburn.

Father's frown was immediate. "Have you seen him again?"

"Oh, no," I said. "Not since we spoke outside his little camp."

Father shook his head. "A stranger was prowling around when you were in Aberlour, and he was probably the same man."

"He could be entirely innocent," Mother tried to keep the

peace. "He may be one of these Romantic poets who like to look at the wild scenery and so on."

"I'll give him bloody Romantic scenery." Father forgot his resolve not to swear in front of his children and proceeded to go into great detail about exactly where he would stuff the romantic scenery.

"Poor Ensign Hepburn," I said.

"What the devil has Ensign Hepburn got to do with anything?" Father growled.

I realised that I was again thinking of quite the wrong stranger. "Oh," I said. "You mean that man who was walking on An Bodach last night."

"Who the devil else would I mean?"

I caught my mother's eye as I looked away. She raised her eyebrows, and I knew she would be asking me searching questions later when Father was not in the house. I had forgotten about that other stranger. My thoughts about Ensign Hepburn and the happenings in Mr Snodgrass's office had chased that solitary sighting right out of my mind.

※

As always, the night was happy with all my brothers and sisters crowding into the house. I shared a box bed with three sisters while my brothers crammed into another, and Mother and Father had one all to themselves.

They had a bit of privacy behind a curtain, but I still heard them talking together and Father's deep laugh combined with Mother's lighter giggle. I envied them their happiness and wondered if I would indeed ever get a man for myself.

With that thought and young Caitlin spooned in front of me, I thought again of Ensign Andrew Hepburn and his freckles that merged when he smiled. And then I thought of Mr Gillespie's soft drawling accent, and then I fell asleep.

A ceilidh is a cross between a smoking concert and a dance,

where everything goes. There is music and laughter and drinking and dancing. Everybody can take part, and everyone is welcome, all ages, young and old, and the music lasts all night and usually well into the next day. Sometimes it can last for quite a few days as the pipers or accordion players or fiddlers fall asleep and wake up and start all over again.

There are usually a few arguments and an occasional fight, but the participants expect such things, and nobody takes them seriously. We are all friends in a few moments. The whisky flows free, and often, nine months or so later, a few new babies pop out to grace the glen. That is the way of life, and nobody expects anything else.

I was quite looking forward to this ceilidh. As the oldest of the family, I had pride of place on the chair as Mother did my hair and ensured that I looked my best. It was not the greatest of bests, for I was not a beautiful girl. I had the Gunn handsome features rather than any classic prettiness, with a strong chin and my father's bold eyes. Boys tended to treat me with wary respect rather than adoration, despite my lack of inches. Certainly, I had no circle of admirers such as Catriona MacRae or Eilidh Mackay. Catriona was my friend while Eilidh was the darling one of the glen which made all the men admire her and the girls jealous. The Gunn brood perched on creepie-stools, or sat cross-legged on the floor, or stood to watch as Mother did my hair. It was nothing fancy, nothing that compared to the city styles of Edinburgh of London or Paris. However, people from those places don't have to sit amid peat smoke with the cattle from the adjoining byre lowing as a background and a single oval pier-glass as the only aide. Nor do they have six children giving loud comments and poking fun all the time.

Twice I had to rise from my chair to slap a cheeky young head and once to skelp a plump little bottom to keep the owner quiet. And all the time, Father was standing with a slight smile on his face, enjoying his family.

After my exertions, poor Mother had to start on my hair all

over again. She had the patience of a saint, that woman, until somebody went a little too far and she lost her temper and cleared the cottage of everybody except me.

The Gunns are a fertile, passionate breed, but we also have a temper fit to quieten the devil. Even Father fled when Mother was on the warpath.

When Mother had calmed down and finished, my auburn-brown hair was as pretty as it ever could be. She had braided it in front and plaited it behind in a fashion very much like the ancient Greeks. When I thought she had finished, Mother bound everything in place with a snood.

"That'll do, Mother," I said, impatient quinie that I was as I stood away from the pier-glass that was Mother's second pride and joy next to her table.

"Not yet!" She gave me a cuff on my rather prominent behind, which was her way of showing affection as much as a rebuke. "You must look your best for Niall." She pushed me back onto the chair.

As I tutted in exasperation, Mother produced a long strip of blue velvet and tied it low on my forehead, finishing the effect with a tight bow beneath my plait at the back.

"There now." Mother stood back to admire her handiwork. "That's it done. You'll be quite the belle of the ball, and if Niall does not fall over himself to claim you, then he doesn't deserve my darling daughter."

I looked in the pier-glass, turning this way and that and I must say that Mother had done a splendid job. As I hinted, I was not the most prepossessing of girls, being short of stature, forward of temper, and wide of hips, but my hair would stand comparison with anybody else's. That included Eilidh Mackay with all her airs, looks, and graces.

Father cracked open the door and peeped his head into the cottage. "Is it safe to return?" He asked, only partly in jest.

One by one, my younger sisters and brothers also thrust their faces in, so the doorway was a mass of tousled shiny hair and wide eyes.

"Oh, come away ben the house," Mother said testily and immediately her home was full again, just the way she liked it.

The music floated through the light rain, making me smile. I loved music, although I was anything but accomplished on the piano or anything else. I was not a complete tyro: I had played the great Highland pipes from time to time, and I could sing as well as most, with the old Gaelic airs my favourites.

As soon as we heard the music, we lifted our skirts higher and quickened our steps. Catriona grinned over at me, with her eyes alight.

"I am after Sandy Cattanach," she said, "and I don't care who knows."

"You'd better be careful with that man Sandy." I skipped lightly over a wide puddle, careful not to get peat-splashes on my legs. "I have heard that he has a way with girls."

"That is what I heard as well," my wild Catriona said. "I hope that all the stories are true, and if they are not, I will make them true!'

As always, we held the ceilidh in the church hall, much to the uneasiness of the minister. Our reverend was a bit of a stickler for Presbyterian fire, hell and brimstone, and neglected the joy of the Bible. Father and he often disputed the Book, with the minister quoting the Old Testament and Father saying he preferred the New, with the passage where Jesus turned water into wine his favourite.

The glen's folk filled the place. I stepped inside the door, stopped, and then looked around me. There were two pipers, and I swear they were both playing different tunes, a fiddler who sat on the table scraping away as if his life depended on it and a woman I did not know strumming a clarsach, the small Gaelic harp.

Of course, I searched for the most handsome of boys and nearly immediately saw Niall Grant, sitting awkwardly beside his younger brother Fergus, a red-haired tyke with a ready grin and a liking for mischief and mayhem.

"There's Niall," Mother pointed out in a voice far too loud for my liking. She pushed me toward him.

Niall looked up, coloured scarlet and looked away at once, which was quite appealing really.

I stepped in the opposite direction, noticed that Catriona was already in company with Sandy Cattanach and found one of the few unoccupied seats. There were only a few actual chairs, and by unspoken agreement, we reserved them for the older members of the glen.

The rest were simple benches, creepie-stools, and a couple of barrels that had been sawed in two and placed on their end. It was one of the latter on which I perched, manoeuvring it to enable me to have the best view of proceedings. I liked to watch before I committed myself.

There was no actual dancing yet. That would begin when the people had drunk sufficient whisky to overcome their shyness. Highlanders are like that— a naturally reticent people who prefer to watch and listen rather than to participate. It can take large quantities of spirits to overcome this shyness and persuade us to take to the floor, but as soon as we are dancing, it is equally hard to get them to stop.

"There's the handsome lad," Mother reminded me. She had brought the whole family, and my brothers and sisters crowded around with encouraging cries.

"I can see him," I said.

"Go on, then," Caitlin shrieked. "Before Catriona or that horrible Eilidh Mackay gets him."

"I'll go when I'm ready," I said and wished them all to Hades or Edinburgh, whichever was furthest away.

"Come on." Mother ushered the siblings away. "We'll leave Fiona in peace. She may have to get used to being on her own unless she gets a move on!" Her look as she left was full of meaning.

With Father involved, there was plenty whisky to go around. Ferintosh, we called it sometimes, but more often it was termed peat reek, the illicitly distilled whisky that Father and half of Scotland made in defiance of the Excise laws. There were other drinks available, with claret and port as well as wine and even some ale.

"Niall!" I heard the name as I wriggled my bottom to get comfortable on my half-barrel. "Niall!"

Eilidh Mackay was different from most girls in the glen. She was slightly younger than me, about nineteen, and nature had placed all her curves just where boys wanted them, and she knew how to play them to best advantage. Eilidh was also clever, far above me in the single-class school we had both attended, and sang like a laverock. In short, she was my nemesis, and I hated her with every fibre of my being and being a Gunn, that is a lot of hatred to carry around with me.

I slid from my barrel, not at all sure what I was going to do as Eilidh glided across the hall. Her white skirt was far too tight around her hips, and her breasts thrust toward poor Niall, whose eyes were attracted to them as naturally as an autumn moth to a candle flame.

Eilidh, being what she was, she had added a bright red ribbon around her waist, with an ornate bow at the back, just above the swell of her hips. As always with Eilidh, luck favoured her. The man next to Niall vacated his seat just as she arrived. She slid into it as naturally as if it had been made for her, favouring its recent occupant with the most radiant smile that God, or the devil, could devise. Within a minute, she was chatting away to Niall, her hands moving and occasionally resting on his arms or even on his leg— the forward hussy.

They had a drink in their hands, with Niall sipping at a tumbler of whisky, perhaps to gain some courage, and Eilidh delicately holding a glass of claret.

Trust Eilidh to choose claret; she probably thought it made her appear sophisticated, the wanton trollop.

Mercifully for my peace of mind, the dancing started then, with couples pairing off and leaping around with immense energy or showing great skill with the complicated footwork necessary for some of the Highland jigs. I sat there in misery for half an hour or so, wondering what to do and watching Mother and Father dancing together, until Seonaid, my sister next to me in age, approached.

"That Eilidh girl's got your Niall," she told me.

"I know," I said.

"Well—" Seonaid poked me in true sisterly fashion. "Go and get him back."

"I don't know how," I said. For, in truth, I was more than a little in awe of Eilidh and her looks and talent. I was the least good-looking of my Mother's children and the least favoured in height as well. In my case, the runt of the litter came first.

"Do you want him back?" Seonaid asked.

Well, now, that was the crucial question. I had not been unduly concerned about Niall when I entered the hall. If I had, I would have sat near him, but after watching Eilidh making sheep's eyes at him, my position had altered quite a lot, and I wanted his company. It was as much to spite Eilidh as anything else.

"Yes, I do want him back," I said.

Seonaid grinned. She was her father's daughter that one, and up to all the tricks in creation. "Leave it to us," she said.

I sat back on my barrel, caught Mother's eye, and gave a weak smile as she nodded her head toward Niall and mouthed urgent encouragement.

The pipers had combined to play the same tune now, and somebody had produced a pair of broadswords from God-knows-where, so Father and one of the old soldiers were showing the sword dance, with their bare feet nimble between the shining blades laid on the floor.

Everybody was watching the dancing when there came the most almighty crash from the opposite side of the hall, where

Niall and Eilidh were. I looked over in time to see Eilidh fall flat on her back with her legs in the air.

As in those days. Highland women seldom wore underthings; Eilidh subjected us to a genuinely scandalous sight of bare legs and other parts. I stared in mixed concern and amusement, and then Seonaid and three of my little brothers burst out from the shelter of the benches, grinning and giggling fit to burst.

It was not hard to work out what had happened. One of my little monsters had looped the bow at the back of Eilidh's skirt around a chair. When Eilidh stood, the chair had dragged her back, and she had fallen. As she had been holding a glass, the contents had spilt over her. Now she was wet, bedraggled, and disgraced in front of everybody. It was a sight to gladden my heart.

"Eilidh," I said, rushing across to help her, all false concern and hidden amusement. "Eilidh, are you hurt?" I helped her up. "Niall, straighten these chairs up, please. Thank you." I gave poor Niall my best smile and eased Eilidh down, maliciously pleased to see that her drink had spilt onto the seat, so she rested her shapely rump in a pool of red claret that would thoroughly stain her white skirt. I hoped she was infernally uncomfortable as the claret soaked through the thin material. "Oh, you poor thing," I said, pressing her bottom down firmly into the puddle. "Here, let me help."

"It's all right," Eilidh said, trying to raise herself from that most vexing pool of claret. "I'm not hurt."

"I'm so glad to hear that," I lied, pawing at the red stain on the front of her dress so that it spread further and rubbing with a cloth that Niall most obligingly found for me.

"Just look at your dress!" Mrs Mackay arrived at her daughter's side, thin-lipped and with her brow furrowed. "You've spoiled it, positively spoiled it."

That was what I hoped to hear. "It will clean up," I said, rubbing furiously to enlarge the damage.

"No!" Mrs Mackay gave Eilidh a cuff on the head, presumably

to cheer her up. "You clumsy child! Get home. Get home at once."

I watched with glee as Eilidh stood up, immediately displaying the brilliant claret stain that had spread across her rump.

"Oh!" Mrs Mackay said and hustled her daughter out of the hall.

There was a subdued buzz of conversation, and then somebody signalled to the fiddler.

"Right, Wullie," a man called, and the music began again.

The incident was soon forgotten, save for some amusement, and I was free to pursue Niall.

"You were very kind to Eilidh," Niall said. He had no sisters and apparently believed my act.

"She needed help," I said. "The poor thing looked utterly woebegone as she lay there on the ground with her dress around her hips." I thought it best to remind Niall how foolish Eilidh had looked. "It would have melted a heart of stone."

Niall shook his head. "I thought that you two were not friends, yet you were first to come and help her."

"We're not close friends," I told him. "But I don't like to see anybody suffering like that. It must have been embarrassing for her to display her legs as she did. No respectable man will wish to know her now." I shook my head as I played my cards one by one. "Indeed, I think that any man who goes out with her again will be tainted. People will remember poor Eilidh as the hussy who displayed herself at the ceilidh."

"Oh." Niall had to think about that. "Poor Eilidh."

"Poor Eilidh indeed," I sympathised. "And pity the poor man who lands her as a wife. How everybody will laugh at him."

He coloured at that, and I dried the seat of the chair that Eilidh had vacated. "There. That's better." I smiled at him. He was slightly more handsome than I remembered, with light brown hair that flopped across one eye. "She will be all right," I said. "You should not believe all the stories that people tell about her."

"Which stories?" Niall asked.

As I was about to rip Eilidh's character to shreds, shouting distracted me, and I looked up.

"That's your father's voice," Niall said.

I listened for a few moments; I was sure that Father could handle any sort of trouble that the glen could throw at him, and I expected the noise to calm down in a few moments. Instead, it increased. Most of the people turned to the outside door, and even the pipers stopped playing to listen. They did not stop drinking, though. Highland pipers need their drink.

"We'd better go and have a look," Niall said.

Others had the same idea, blocking my passage to the door. It was Niall who pushed through and dragged me behind him. "Come on, Fiona."

At first, I could see only the crowd of men and hear their shouting and swearing, and then I saw that Father was in the middle of them.

"What's happening?" I shouted. "That's my father there! Let me through! Father, what are you doing?"

"It's a bloody Exciseman!" father was shouting. "He's an Exciseman, a gauger! Give him hell, boys! He's been spying on us these last few days."

I saw the figure lying on the ground, with two of the glensmen kicking at his prostrate body, and I gasped with astonishment.

"Leave him be!" I shouted. "Leave him!" Pushing myself through, and without thinking what I was doing, I shoved Donnie Grant, Niall's father, out of the way and crouched down beside the man on the ground.

"Kick him again, Donnie!" Iain Mackay, Eilidh's brother, yelled. "Teach the gaugers what happens to them in Glen nan Gall."

"Mr Gillespie!" I crouched beside the prostrate man. "It's me. It's Fiona Gunn."

I looked around at the circle of faces. I had known these men all my life. I had grown up with their daughters, brothers, sisters, and sons, and here they were acting like bullies.

"Get away!" I yelled. "Leave this man alone."

Mr Gillespie took hold of my arm. "Miss Gunn," he spoke in a hoarse whisper. "Don't tell them who I am."

"But I must," I said.

"It would oblige me if you did not," Mr Gillespie said.

I stood beside Mr Gillespie. "Leave this man alone," I said. "He is not a gauger."

"Stand aside, Fiona," Father said. "We know best how to handle creatures like this."

"You will not touch him!" I was shaking with a mixture of fear and anger.

"Fiona," Niall spoke more reasonably than anybody there. "You will get hurt for the sake of a stranger. Step aside." He raised his voice. "Fiona is only trying to help," he said.

"He was listening to our conversation," Iain Mackay said. He was as handsome as his sister was beautiful and with the same purposeful attitude. "What he heard can injure everyone in the glen, Fiona, including your family."

"Family is everything," Niall reminded me. "Family is much greater than any stranger."

Niall was correct, of course. I could not go against the wishes of my father and all my friends, cousins and kin. At the same time, I would not step aside and allow them to attack this innocent man.

I set my chin in its most stubborn mode. "You cannot hurt a helpless man," I said. "I will not let you."

"You will not *let* us?" Iain Mackay said in derision, and then the men stepped forward.

I do not know what would have happened if there had not been an interruption. Presumably, the men of the glen would have swept me aside and taken Mr Gillespie to whatever fate they had in mind. Instead, there was an intimidating shout.

"Stop there! Stand aside!"

IN MARCHED ENSIGN HEPBURN AND A DOZEN OF HIS militiamen, muskets held at their shoulders and bayonets gleaming in the light from the hall windows.

4

For a moment, everything seemed to stand still. I was beside Mr Gillespie, facing my father and many of my kin, with these militiamen barging in like some blood-red presence, with Ensign Hepburn at their head. He was every bit as young as I remembered him, with that same freckled face, but now his jaw was set, and he had a look of determination that was very interesting.

"What's going on here?" Strangely, Ensign Hepburn looked at me rather than at Mr Gillespie or my father.

"Nothing to concern the army," Mr Gillespie answered for me. He rose to his feet, winced, and wiped the blood from his face. "It was just a small altercation."

"All right, then," Ensign Hepburn touched the brim of his shako in what may have been a salute. "If you are certain, we'll be getting along."

"Oh, do stay, Ensign Hepburn," I said. Whatever Mr Gillespie thought, I knew my father and the men of the glen. This small altercation could turn into something a lot more serious the moment the militiamen marched away. I saw the mixture of confusion and something else— pleasure perhaps— on Ensign Hepburn's face.

"Oh, Miss Gunn." He hesitated with that appealing uncertainty momentarily returning. "No, Miss Gunn. I have my duty to perform."

"There's no need for the army," Mr Gillespie said. "I just happened to be passing. I'll be on my way. You carry on with whatever it was you were doing, Ensign."

"Oh, yes." Ensign Hepburn looked at me. "We are just a routine picket, sir. We're searching for whisky smugglers, don't you know."

I was glad to see that Father and most of the men had drifted back to the church hall, and the music had restarted.

"You won't find much smuggling at a ceilidh," Mr Gillespie said. "There might be some whisky drinking, though."

Once again, Ensign Hepburn looked at me as if for reassurance. His earlier confidence seemed to have evaporated. "Whisky drinking is not against the law." He decided. "I'll be on my way, then."

As the militia marched into the night, Mr Gillespie smiled. "Thank you, Miss Gunn," he said. "That could have been unpleasant."

"The men thought you were somebody else." I tried to make excuses. "They did not know who you were." I dabbed at the blood that still flowed down his face. "You're bleeding."

The music and laughter increased as people returned to the ceilidh with the incident outside forgotten. I knew my people; they would live for the minute and forget all about the man they had attacked until sobriety brought reason and remorse.

"It's hardly anything," Mr Gillespie said and promptly collapsed.

I stared at him for a moment, unsure what to do. It was full dark; I was temporarily alienated from my family and alone with a stranger who happened to be the new landowner. He was also lying on the ground in a useless, crumpled heap.

"Come on." I crouched at his side as the rain began to fall. "We'll get you somewhere." But where? I could hardly take him to our house. What would Father say? "Where are you staying, Mr Gillespie? Is it at the Inn?"

There was only one Inn nearby. Known as the King's House, it stood by the road that led north to the Laigh of Moray and was about five miles away. I thought it a dreary, desolate building, dirty outside and in, with little cheer for the traveller. I contemplated helping Mr Gillespie over five miles of moorland and hill to this solitary place and hoped he would recover soon.

"Tigh na h-Iolaire." Mr Gillespie intoned the Gaelic without a taste of the English. He spoke the language like a native. "Do you know it?"

Of course, I knew it. I knew everywhere in the glen. "It's been empty for years," I said. "Nobody lives there. The name means the House of the Eagles, and we call it the Big House."

"I know what it means," Mr Gillespie said. "And I live there." He took another step, staggered, and would have fallen again if he had not clutched at me for support.

"Oh." I held him upright, feeling the lean muscle. "If you're sure you wish to go there." I wondered if I should call for help. Who would help a stranger in the rain? Good Samaritans were rather scarce in Glen nan Gall. I looked around, hopeful that Mr Gillespie had a horse with him.

"I came on foot," he said, reading my mind.

"Come on then." I put my arm around his back, wishing that I had never interfered. I had rather been enjoying that ceilidh and the company of Niall. I had hoped to wean him away from that dreadful Eilidh Mackay with her curves and cleverness.

At one time, a path ran from our clachan of Penrioch to the House of the Eagles. We knew it as the Old Road and could still trace it as an overgrown track that skirted the long rigs where we planted our crops and the fields where we grazed our hardy cattle.

"Come on, then." I was not the most gracious of helpers as we limped along the Old Road, staggering over ragged tufts of heather and more than once tumbling into muddy holes. The rain increased as we walked, so we were both soaked through long before we reached the skeletal remains of the big house, where there was neither light nor heat to welcome us in.

"Is anybody at home?" I asked, nervous about approaching the building.

"Only me," Mr Gillespie said.

The Big House was precisely that, a big house. Three storeys high, time had long shattered the glass in most of the windows while a series of stone steps led to the heavy front door, tall and wide enough to accommodate a man on horseback, let alone a girl from the glen.

I glanced at the weather-battered carving above the door, the eagle with outspread wings holding three arrows that gave the house its name.

"I use a side door," Mr Gillespie told me. "This way." He fumbled in his pocket and produced a key that was as large as my hand.

"I will leave you here," I said, very nervous about walking into an empty house with a strange man. I might've been a naïve country girl, but I was not stupid.

"I'll be all right now," Mr Gillespie said. "I'll manage. Thank you for your help."

I slid my supporting arm away. Mr Gillespie took two steps and fell again.

Sighing, I hauled him up. "Come on, then."

Reasoning that a man in such a weak condition would not be a threat, I helped him open a smaller door at the side of the house, and we stepped inside. I must admit to feeling more than a little trepidation, for we had always avoided the Big House. That was where the landowner had traditionally lived. Other glens had chiefs and chieftains and clan this and clan that. Not our glen. We were Glen nan Gall, the Glen of Strangers, and it was many years— probably many centuries— since a clan chief ruled our glen.

"Wait, please," Mr Gillespie said. "I have a tinder box here."

The smell of damp was unpleasant. Mr Gillespie scraped a spark and applied it to the wick of a candle. Yellow light pooled around us, illuminating wood-panelled walls and wooden floorboards.

"There we are." He lifted the candle so shadows danced along a ceiling fancier than any I had ever seen in my life.

"Which way?" I looked along the length of a corridor.

"This way," Mr Gillespie said, and I helped him through a doorway that led into another corridor. Cobwebs hid the ceiling, and something furry with sharp little claws ran across my bare feet.

There was another door, and we entered a large room without a single iota of furniture except a shakedown bed in one corner and the most ornate chair that I had ever seen in my life. Behind the bed was a bundle, such as tinkers or such-like carry. The same eagle symbol decorated the fireplace.

" Is this where you live?" I looked around for some sign of creature comfort. There was none.

"Just lay me on the bed, and I'll be better by tomorrow." Mr Gillespie said.

I had a look at him. Muddy and with his clothes torn, he looked more like an orphan of the storm than the owner of a Highland glen. "You need to clean up," I decided, more my mother's daughter than I had realised. "Do you have water?"

I found a well in a small courtyard at the back of the house, with an old-fashioned wooden bucket on the end of a rope. I brought some water into the house and saw Mr Gillespie collapsed on the chair, softly groaning as if he was in the last extremities of life.

Leaving him to his own devices, I gathered some of the dry sticks that were plentiful in the house and started a small fire in the grate. Mr Gillespie remained on the chair, bloody and bruised, with the occasional slight sound of pain.

I sighed, unsure what to do. Normally I would have asked my mother for help, and the family would have gathered around with ready hands and advice, but that was not possible in these circumstances. I was alone, with a strange, injured man. I took a deep breath. The first thing I had to do was discover the extent of his injuries.

"Right, Mr Gillespie," I made myself sound as confident as possible. "I'm going to wash the blood from your face and then have a look at you and see if you have broken anything."

I wanted warm water as well as the heat from the fire. It was only September, but already there was a chill in the air, and I did not know how hardy Mr Gillespie was, despite his size and weather-beaten appearance. Fortunately, there was a metal pot beside the bed, and I poured some water into this and placed it on the fire. Mr Gillespie was watching me in between bouts of unconsciousness.

"All right." I searched for a cloth, sighed, and tore a strip from my petticoat. It was my only petticoat, mind you, and I resolved to ask Mr Gillespie to buy me another as soon as he was fit again. I had seen his gold, and he could well afford it, blast his impudence in getting himself injured. And blast Father and his friends for attacking the poor man and causing me all this bother.

I soaked the linen in the barely warm water and began to wash the dried blood from Mr Gillespie's face. He gave a little smile. "It has been a long time since anybody did that," he said.

"Where are you hurting?" I asked. He had a long face, deeply tanned by sun or wind, with the brightest of blue eyes and a mouth he set in a hard line, either through pain or natural grimness.

Mr Gillespie frowned. "My head," he said. "My ribs and my legs."

"You have a cut on your head and some bruises," I told him. "It's not serious. It will feel better tomorrow, although the bruises may spread. As for the rest, let's have a look. Off with your jacket and shirt."

"I can't do that." Mr Gillespie showed surprising delicacy for a man in pain.

"Oh, don't be silly," I tried to sound bright and cheerful. "I have three brothers."

"Maybe so," Mr Gillespie said. "I am not one of them."

"None of your nonsense now," I used my best eldest-sister voice. "Off with it. Come on. I'll help you."

He was lean and hard under his shirt, with well-defined muscles and not an ounce of fat. He was also quite severely bruised above the marks of older wounds. I wondered how many of these injuries my father had caused.

"You've been in the wars," I remarked as I traced the tip of my finger down a long white scar.

"Yes," Mr Gillespie said.

"This may hurt a little," I said. A few years ago, Hector, my middle brother, had fallen over a crag while searching for bird eggs to add to our diet. He had broken two ribs and made a lot less fuss than Mr Gillespie did about a few minor bumps. "I'm going to press your ribs one by one to see if you have broken any."

"All right," Mr Gillespie said, visibly bracing himself for immediate pain.

I pushed lightly on his chest, feeling for the give of a broken bone and expecting Mr Gillespie to leap and yell if I found one. He was braver than I had anticipated and only made little gasping sounds, which encouraged me to press a little harder.

"Easy," he said, attempting to push my hand away.

"Nothing broken," I said cheerfully. "If there had been, you would soon have let me know." I looked again. "A few bruises and a minor abrasion, nothing to worry about. Now, where on your leg does it hurt?" I hoped it was not too far up.

"My ankle," Mr Gillespie said and eased that worry.

"Let's have a look then." I knelt at his feet. "Which one?"

"The left one."

I eased off his boot and pulled down his stocking. His foot was white, and his ankle undoubtedly swollen.

"I see," I said, running my hand over it.

With three active brothers, I was quite used to looking for injuries and knew the difference between play-acting and genuine hurt. Although Mr Gillespie's head and ribs were superficial knocks that none of my brothers would even have noticed, let alone complained about, the ankle looked genuinely, if only slightly, damaged.

"Aye," I said. "Does this hurt?" Taking hold of his foot and expecting his howls of protest, I wriggled it from side to side.

He pulled it away. "Ow! Yes!"

"It's not broken," I said. "It might be twisted or sprained. Do you have anything in the house I can use as a bandage to bind it up?" I was loath to use any more of my undergarments to nurse this weakling of a man.

"I've only got what you see." Mr Gillespie waved his hand in the direction of his bundle.

"Oh." That was discouraging. I rummaged through the meagre collection; there was a long knife and some spare clothing that was far too coarse to use as a bandage and half a loaf of stale bread. "I'll have to find something else. Stay here and don't move or watch me."

"I'm not going anywhere," Mr Gillespie said with what might have been a smile.

Stepping out of that room, I slipped off my petticoat, sighed, and returned. "Now, no funny business, mind."

Mr Gillespie smiled again. "Of course not, Miss Gunn." His eyes followed me as I unsheathed his knife. The blade was cared for, sharp and well-used. Steeling myself, I slit my only petticoat into long strips. "Let's see your ankle again."

Crouching in front of him, I placed his heel on my knee and bound his ankle rather tightly. He remained still.

"Good boy," I said. "Now, what do you have to eat in the house?"

"Nothing." Mr Gillespie admitted. "Only that bit bread there. I was on my way to the Inn when I heard the music and wandered over."

"That was our ceilidh," I said. "You would have been better continuing to the Inn. The folk of the glen don't take kindly to strangers."

"So I noticed," Mr Gillespie said.

"Strangers have a habit of causing trouble." I tried to excuse my father and his friends for attacking this unfortunate man.

"They thought I was an Exciseman," Mr Gillespie said.

"That is correct."

"Is there much illicit whisky-making here?"

"How should I know the answer to that?" I avoided his question.

"You strike me as the sort of young woman who would know everything," Mr Gillespie said.

Unsure if Mr Gillespie was insulting or complimenting me, I bowed my head and changed the subject. "You need to eat something to keep your strength up," I said. "I'll be back in an hour."

I knew that the ceilidh would continue through the night and well into the next day, at least, so nobody would see me when I returned to the clachan. Penrioch was a reasonably large township with a dozen houses, four enclosures for the cattle and a corn-drying kiln. The rain continued as I ran to our house and robbed my mother's store of food, bundling it into a plaid to protect it from the wet as I ran back. My feet splashed through the mud.

Mr Gillespie sat precisely where I had left him.

"Here," I said. "I have flour and oatmeal and crowdie, with whisky and some sphagnum moss." I was not in the best of tempers after passing the happy sounds of the ceilidh twice while I walked through the rain and entirely ruined my carefully contrived hair. I thought of Niall alone in there and wondered which girl would pick up where I left off. "Let me see that cut on your head."

I must confess that I was not the most gentle of nurses as I examined poor Mr Gillespie's wounds again and applied sphagnum moss to them. "This moss cleans the wound and also stops the bleeding," I told Mr Gillespie. "You can hold it in place. It is also useful for other purposes." I let him wonder what I meant as I busied myself in making food.

I added water to the oatmeal and placed the mixture on the fire, pouring in a little whisky for flavouring. "I will make a few of these cakes," I said. "It is wholesome and long-lasting."

"Thank you." Mr Gillespie said as I gave him instructions on how to make oatmeal cakes.

"The flour is for bannocks," I said, handing over some of Mother's precious store of salt. I knew I would be in trouble when Mother found out that I had raided her larder, but one must endure such things.

"I'll come back from time to time and ensure you are all right," I said, deciding that I had wasted sufficient time with this useless man.

"Thank you." Mr Gillespie looked very lonely in that dark room. "Why are you so kind to me?"

"You helped me with the Factor," I said.

Mr Gillespie smiled. "That was nothing," he said.

"It was a lot more than nothing to me." I hesitated, torn between remaining in this cold room with this stranger and returning to the ceilidh. Sighing, I knew I could not abandon the helpless man to the chill and scoured that floor of the House of Eagles, gathering wood for the fire. "That should keep you warm for a while," I said as I finally left him.

He did not reply. He had fallen asleep on the chair. Such is the gratitude of kings and landowners in this Scotland. It is best to avoid both.

5

I saw the movement from afar. The bustle of men through the early-morning dim accompanied the clatter of equipment and the hoarse barking of orders in the English language. Slipping behind a rock, I crouched and listened, trying to make sense of what was happening.

There was the gleam of light as somebody put flame to a lantern, and I saw a score of men in militia uniforms together with a tall man I could not make out and a smaller figure that I could've sworn was a woman. The orders came again, and one of the militia lifted something from the ground and held it high.

I gasped; the militia had discovered one of Father's black bothies, as we called the illicit distilleries, and were either wrecking the equipment or taking it away, I could not be sure which. Keeping low and quiet, I crept closer, uncaring of the mud and damage to my best clothes, for there was nothing that a wash or a needle and thread could not cure.

Light now pooled from half a dozen lanterns, revealing the faces of the militia. That hard-faced Captain Barrow was in command, together with a civilian in a tall beaver-skin hat whose long cloak swept the ground as he walked. As I watched, I could see that the civilian was in overall command for he spoke to the captain, who then gave orders to the soldiers.

"Father will not be pleased," I said to myself as the militia removed the hard-to-replace worm, the copper stillhead, and the perforated iron plate on which Father dried the malt.

It seemed that the Exciseman, for the tall civilian could be no other, had waited until the men of the glen were all at the ceilidh before they struck. Things were changing in the Glen of Strangers, and not for the better.

"But what most concerns me—" Father said when I told him the news as soon as he had sobered, two days or so later— "is how the gauger and the militia knew exactly where to find my still?"

"Remember I saw that man watching from Am Bodach," I said. "He must have been the gauger."

"I'm convinced he was the man you rescued from us," Father said. "The fellow you say is the new landowner."

"It was not Mr Gillespie," I said, too quickly. "He is injured and could not possibly have come."

I felt the penetrating look of both Mother and Father as they analysed my words. "How do you know so much about him?" Mother asked.

I took a deep breath. "After Father beat him up," I said. "I took him home. I could not leave him to lie in the moorland, all battered and bruised. He may have died."

"And a damned good thing if he did," Father said. "It would be better that a stranger died rather than he destroyed my still. That's our livelihood, you know, Fiona."

"I know that," I snapped back, unsure if Father was accusing me of leading the Excisemen to the distillery.

"It is as well that I have others," Father said. "Tell me all that you saw. Every detail."

He listened as I described what I had seen, nodding as I mentioned the part the militia had played and frowning when I spoke of the woman I had seen.

"This woman," Mother said, "what was she like?"

"I am not sure," I said. "I did not see her properly. She wore a hooded cloak."

"How old? How tall? What colour of hair?" Mother fired the questions in quite as abrupt a manner as the Exciseman had given his orders, and I was hard-pressed to keep up with her.

"How old? I did not see, but she stood very erectly. I would say she was about five foot five, but her hood covered her head, so I did not see her hair."

Mother frowned, tapping her fingers on the table around which we all sat. "I don't like this mention of a woman," she said. "We have dealt with Excisemen before, and I know that you, Calum, will handle him by and by. The militia will be a threat with their pickets, but you will have men watching them."

"I already have," Father said. "They won't be able to do anything without my lads telling me."

"This Exciseman seems to be active and dangerous," Mother said. "You can try bribes to keep them away; that usually works."

Father nodded. "As long as it is not Malcolm Campbell."

The name put a chill in our home. Malcolm Campbell was the most notorious of all the gaugers, a man who had put more smugglers and distillers into jail than any other ten of his kind. I had heard that he had a score of wounds on his body after fights with distillers and had shot or stabbed at least five men.

"We will have to be very careful," Mother said. "And watch out for this woman." She looked at me as a sudden thought came to her. "Fiona, the day the militia arrived, you saw a flash on the hillside, like the sun reflecting on glass, and later you saw the figure of a man on Am Bodach."

"That's right," I agreed.

"Could it have been a woman on the hill? It was dark. Perhaps it was a woman spying on the glen."

I screwed up my face, trying to remember. "It may have been," I said. "It may have been a tall woman."

Mother nodded. "I'll pass the word around, although if any strange women come into the glen, we will soon know about it. I'll check with Ellen at the Inn."

Father kissed me on the tip of my nose, a sure sign that he had forgiven me. "You were a brave lass standing up for that fellow outside the ceilidh," he said.

"He was not the Exciseman," I said for at least the tenth time. "That was Mr Gillespie. He's the new owner of the glen."

Father smiled. "Well then, he will soon go the same way as his predecessors."

"You had better be careful tomorrow, Calum," Mother said. "Remember that there are soldiers in Dunbeiste now."

Father gave his usual broad grin. "I'm not concerned about the South Edinburgh Militia," he said. "I doubt they will even see us, yet along interfere." He hitched up his plaid and checked the pistol he wore at his belt. "We'll be back in three days, or four at the most."

"Calum," Niall Grant pushed into our house, his face worried. "It's Sandy Cattanach."

"What about Sandy," Father said. "Is he late again?"

"Worse," Niall shook his head. "He's gone down sick with something. He can't make it."

As I wondered if Sandy's sickness had anything to do with an urgent desire to pleasure Catriona, Father again forgot my presence and swore softly.

"We need Sandy," he said. "It's too late to find somebody else."

Mother looked at me and raised her eyebrows. "I know somebody who would like to come along" she said. "I know somebody who knows the hills as well as anybody else and who has a point to prove to get back into your good books."

"There is nobody out of my good books," Father said.

He was telling the truth. Although he possessed a quick

temper, he was also quick to forgive and forgot yesterday's trespasses with the dawn.

"All the same, Fiona could be useful." Mother gave me a little push forward. She lowered her voice to a whisper. "Niall is going, it's a good chance to make up with him and cut Eilidh out completely."

"What would I be doing?" I had never been on one of Father's smuggling expeditions, although I knew what he did.

"You would be leading a garron," Father said.

And leading a garron was what I was doing two hours later when we left Glen nan Gall and mounted Bealach na Ba— the pass of the cattle. There were a dozen garrons, the sturdy Highland pony of the hills— fourteen men of the glens and me. Each garron held two kegs or four nine-gallon *pigeadh* – jars – of peat reek, the illegally distilled whisky that was the plague of the government and the saviour of the Highlands. The coming dark hid us from the garrison of Dunbeiste only a quarter of a mile to the west.

"There is the famous South Edinburgh Militia," Father mocked. "Here to curb the whisky smugglers." He patted the rump of the nearest garron. "Here we are, lads! Come and get us."

There was a growling laugh from my fellow smugglers. We carried on, mounting the ancient pass up which reivers and drovers had driven their cattle for hundreds of years.

I was in the middle, leading my laden garron as we mounted that pass step by step with the wind rising with every yard we climbed. When we reached the summit, I looked down over the glen. I saw the burn of Allt Gobhlach– the forked burn– glint silver in the moonlight, with the greater sheen of Gorm Loch, the Blue Loch from which it flowed. I saw the pinpricks of lights from the clachan of Penrioch and imagined my mother and siblings there, worrying about Father and me.

I also saw the lanterns on the walls of Dunbeiste swinging in the breeze, and, despite my family loyalty, I thought of Ensign Hepburn with his freckles and open, friendly grin.

"Fiona!" Niall Grant's voice broke my reverie. "Who was that man you defended the other night?"

I jerked my mind away from Ensign Hepburn. "That was Mr Gillespie," I said. "He is the new landowner."

"He would be the man who sent the gaugers and soldiers after our still." Niall loomed up to me, frowning.

Up here in the hills, he looked completely different from the diffident boy at the ceilidh. Here he was in his element, a man among men, and I was the outsider, the newcomer to the smuggling trade. Being my father's daughter counted for nothing tonight, and I had to prove myself to these hardy men of the heather.

"I do not know," I said honestly. "I do know that Mr Gillespie was alone against a dozen. That is not right."

"You defended an outsider, a stoorie-foot against the glen." Niall was hot with anger.

"What was happening was wrong," I said. "I would have done the same for anybody— glensman or incomer."

"Even for a gauger?" Niall injected contempt into his words, and I knew I had to be very careful with my answer. Gaugers were the enemy; they wanted to destroy all our distilleries and put us all out of business.

Since the slow decline of the cattle trade with the great peace of 1815, whisky making was all we had. Without it, we would have only poverty. The young men and women would drift away, and we would be yet another sad glen of desolation like so many others. The 1820s were a bitter time in the Highlands when Clearance was the norm, and landowners drove the people from the glens for their personal benefit and sporting entertainment.

"I would not count a gauger as a person," I mirrored Niall's tone. "They are a different species to humans."

I heard one of the men laugh and realised that everybody had been listening for my response.

"Well said, young Fiona," a rough voice sounded from ahead.

We moved on northwards with my loyalty proved. Gunns do not lie to kin or friends.

The pass eased downward now into a welter of rounded, wind-scoured hills where only my father and a handful of others knew the ways around the treacherous bogs and hidden gulleys that plunged for hundreds of feet into the unseen dark. This hill-country was the land of the wild deer, the golden eagle and the whisky smuggler. Not even Malcolm Campbell would dare to come here. Or if he did, he would not be around to return.

We halted under a yellow moon, with the wind brushing music from the heather and the melody of a burn gurgling on our right.

"We eat now," Father decided, "and rest the garrons."

We ate the cakes of porridge we had brought and lay in the shelter of a rowan tree, careful not to fall asleep lest madness creep in with the caress of the moon.

After a while, Father gave the word, and we set off again, marching with our garrons along tracks that only a hill-man could see.

"So, what were you thinking protecting that stranger?" Niall Grant returned to his previous question.

"I was thinking that he needed some help," I said.

"You went against your kin and the glen." Niall sounded more hurt than angry. "How could you do that?"

"He needed help," I repeated, for, in truth, I could not explain further. I did not know why I had stepped in to help Mr Gillespie, except perhaps what I had already told him. He had helped me with Snodgrass the Factor.

"If he is the landowner, then he must be rich," Niall said.

I thought of Mr Gillespie's bags of gold, and then I remembered his stark room in that shell of a house and laughed. "No," I said, shaking my head. "I do not believe that Mr Gillespie is rich."

"He bought the glen," Niall said. "That must have cost plenty."

"I think it cost him everything he has," I said. "I've seen a gaberlunzie man with better clothes and a blind pauper with more possessions."

"Oh," Niall said. "I thought... "

I waited for him to explain further but instead, he relapsed into silence, although he did look across to me a few times as we walked onwards. Somewhere in the dark, a fox called, the sound lonely. I looked away and smiled.

Well now, Niall, you are wondering, are you not? Did you believe that I was chasing Mr Gillespie for some romantic or financial reason? Now you know better, what are you going to do? Are you going to allow Eilidh to lure you into her warm body that conceals a heart of pure ice? Or are you wondering if I am worth pursuing? Here I am, Niall Grant, chase me until I catch you, if you are worth the catching.

I walked on, enjoying the tension I could feel within Niall and wondering how he compared with my freckled ensign. On the one hand, there was a boy I had known all my life, a loyal enough lad whose life was an open book. We would each fit into the other's lifestyles without any effort, and that would be that. No traumatic changes and a home in the glen, like my mother and my grandmother and generation after generation of Gunns stretching back until the first Gunn arrived here from the far north about the time of the battle of Harlaw.

On the other hand, there was an endearing young man, so shy he could hardly speak at times, but well educated and a gentleman with his slender hands. Ensign Hepburn could introduce me to a whole new world. I would see Edinburgh, the capital city and experience all the glamour known, with balls and soirees and whatever other pleasures else the wife of an officer knew.

Did I intend to become the wife of an officer? Did I think

that highly of Ensign Hepburn?

Would a barefooted Highland girl from the glens fit in down in the South Country?

There was much to consider.

We arrived in the pre-dawn dark, with a bustle of traffic on the roads and lights already a-gleam in a hundred windows. I had never been to Perth before that day. I had thought it would've been like Aberlour, a double row of houses on either side of a broad road. I was wrong. It was a vast city of many streets, with buildings larger than any I could imagine and more people than I thought existed in the entire world.

"Where are we going, Father?" I looked at the town that seemed to swallow me up.

"There is an Inn I know down this road here," Father said.

"I don't like it here." I felt closed in among so many buildings so near together.

"Stay with me, and you'll be fine." Father patted my shoulder. "It's time you saw more of the world."

"I don't want to see more of the world," I said, pressing against Father. "I want to go back home."

"It's all right." Father patted my arm. "Just keep calm. The Inn is just ahead."

It felt strange to be leading a garron through the street of a town, with people gawping at us through half-seen windows and the noise of vehicles growling on roads nearby. The Inn was larger than our Kings House, with a stocky man standing outside, waiting.

"That's David Black," Father said.

Black opened a gate into a courtyard at the back of his Inn. We led our garrons in one by one, and two men quickly unloaded the kegs and carried them inside the Inn.

"Good to see you again, Calum." Black shook my father's

hand as if they were long-lost brothers meeting in the heart of Africa rather than Christians in a Scottish town.

I heard Father and Black talking together and the musical chink of money.

"All right, out we go," Father ordered.

"We've only been ten minutes," I said.

"If anybody sees a whole convoy of garrons in the courtyard, they'll know what's happening," Father explained.

I nodded. We left with some haste, passing along the dark street as we headed to the open country to the north of the town. We had barely made the fields when I saw the tall man approaching on his horse.

"Father." I grabbed Father's arm. "That's him."

There was something about the man that I recognised. I was not sure what it was, perhaps the way he carried himself, the way he walked or the set of his shoulders. I did not know. I only knew that the rider was the same man as I had seen on Am Bruach.

"The Exciseman?"

"I think so."

Father slipped a hand inside his coat, where he had thrust his pistol through the waistband of his trousers.

"Be careful, Father," I said. I did not want to see him hanged for murder.

"I rather think it is the gauger who should be careful," Father spoke in a tone I had never heard before.

The Exciseman kicked in his spurs and hurried towards us. "You, there!" He pointed to Father. "Stop! Stop, I say!"

"Gaelic only, boys," Father said.

"I am Malcolm Campbell," the tall man announced. "I am an officer of His Majesty's Excise."

Father looked at him, smiled and continued walking, with the others following. I pulled my garron on and hoped that Campbell did not try to talk to me.

"Don't you understand the King's English, damn you?"

Campbell spurred in front of Father, turned his horse, and faced him.

Father gave a smile that would have graced an inhabitant of Bedlam and guided the leading garron around the Exciseman.

"That game won't work with me," Campbell said in Gaelic. "I am an officer of His Majesty's Excise, and I order you to stop!"

"Then why didn't you say so, rather than gabbling that south country rubbish?" Father pulled his garron to a halt and held up his hand, so the others in the convoy also stopped. "What can we do for you, Mr Malcolm Campbell?"

"Where are you going?" Campbell touched the long pistol he wore at his belt.

"Glen nan Gall," Father replied at once.

"Why?" The word rapped out.

"I live there," Father said. "Why do you wish to know?"

"Glen nan Gall, a haunt of smugglers and thieves." Campbell wrapped his fist around the butt of his pistol.

"Have you been there?" Father asked pleasantly.

I knew that he also had a hand around his pistol.

"Its reputation is well known," Campbell said.

"Come and visit us," Father said. "And find out for yourself. We will give you a warm welcome."

As warm as the hobs of hell, I thought.

Father was wrapping his threat in sweet words while both men eyed each other up, rather like stags in the rutting season, each wondering if he was more powerful than his opponent.

"Where have you been?" Campbell avoided the invitation.

"Perth," Father said. "And if you step aside, we will be on our way."

"You were carrying illicit whisky."

"I was carrying nothing," Father spoke the truth. The garrons had done all the carrying.

"What is your name?" Campbell tried another tack.

"I am Calum Gunn." Father held his eye for a long moment and then urged on his garron.

"Not so fast!" Campbell dragged the pistol from its holster, only to find that Father was faster.

"You can shoot me," Father said, "and then you will be at odds with all these good people here."

I said nothing as, one by one, all the men in the convoy produced a pistol and pointed it at Campbell, or a stout cudgel, which they tapped meaningfully against the palm of their hand.

The Exciseman swore. "I won't forget you, Gunn."

"That's Mr Gunn to you," Father called after him.

Campbell hauled his horse around and walked it along the length of the convoy, with his eyes taking in the face and features of everybody there. He hesitated when he came close to me, and on an impulse, I looked straight into his eyes, swept back my hair and gave a little curtsey.

"Good day to you, Mr Campbell," I said.

He grunted and kicked in his heels, sending his horse on a trot into town.

"Well said, Fiona." Father's words travelled the length of the convoy. "Good day to you, Mr Campbell!" He roared with laughter, which encouraged the others to join in for where Father led, others followed.

Niall Grant smiled at me. "I was not sure if you were going to tell him everything," he said. "Rather than making him feel a complete fool."

"You are not a subtle man, are you, Niall?" I liked him a little more now.

"Now Campbell will make enquiries at every Inn and public house in Perth," Father said.

"Will he find Mr Black?" I asked.

"I don't think so," Father said. "Black's been in this business for years. He'll have a whole selection of hideaways. More importantly, we know that it is Campbell that's hunting us."

"He always gets results," Niall sounded worried.

"Glen nan Gall has a habit of looking after itself," Father said. "The results he gets may not be the results that he wishes."

6

"Go and scout ahead, Niall," Father said as we approached the southern end of Bealach nan Bo. "I would not put it past the Militiamen to be searching for us."

"We are not carrying whisky," Niall said.

"They have found one of our stills," Father said. "There is nothing to prevent them saying that we were carrying whisky on our garrons."

"Ensign Hepburn would not do that," I said.

"Perhaps not." Father did not comment on my knowledge of the freckled ensign. He would ask me later. "Captain Barrow would."

I nodded. "I think that you are right." I had taken a dislike to the captain.

"Off you go, Niall." Father nodded, and Niall disappeared up the pass, keeping off the path so nobody could see him.

"Niall's a good lad," Father said. "You could do a lot worse."

"Thank you, Father." I tried to keep the sarcasm from my voice. "I will find a man when I am ready."

"You're ready now." Father's eyes were busy, with his gaze

running up and down my body before it settled on my face. "At your age, your mother already had you and Lachlan."

"I know," I said. "Mother chose a good man. I will not jump into marriage with just anybody. I want a husband at least half as good as you are."

See what you make of that, Father, dear.

Father grunted. I had hoped that flattery might deceive him.

"Don't wait too long or Fiona or Eilidh will snap him up. You don't want to be left as an old maid."

"I won't be," I said with more conviction than I felt. I did not admit that I had never met a man that matched my father in personality. On the other hand, I did not wish the obnoxious Eilidh to steal Niall if he was in any way suitable.

"Calum!" Niall shouted.

Since we started this expedition, Niall Grant had grown in confidence, or perhaps he was happier out on the heather than in the glen. I watched as he ran down the pass, leaping over stray boulders and avoiding patches of sphagnum moss that concealed peat-holes and boggy ground.

"What's happening, Niall?"

"You were right. The militia is waiting on the other side of the pass." Niall took a deep breath. "I don't know how many."

Father held up his hand, and the column halted. "Tell me exactly what you saw."

"I smelled them first," Niall said. "Somebody was smoking a pipe. So I went to the side and saw them waiting."

"All right, Niall." Father's grin was white in the night. "You did well. Show me."

Leaving the rest of us on the path, Father and Niall hurried to the head of the pass. They returned fifteen minutes later, with Father still smiling and Niall with a bemused look on his face.

"Gather round," Father commanded quietly. "There are a dozen militiamen just beyond the crest of the pass there. We can go round them, which will take an hour or so, or we can show the militia that they cannot trifle with us."

"Show them that we are the Glen nan Gall boys," somebody said, and the others agreed in a quiet growl that raised the hair on the back of my head. I had never heard my neighbours sound like that before. One does not know people until one sees them in adversity.

"What are we going to do, Father?" I asked.

"You are going to stay here and look after the garrons," Father said. "We'll hobble them so they don't stray."

I watched as the men attached *buarachs*— hobbles that ensured they could not take full steps— to the garrons' legs.

"What are you going to do, Father?"

"Things that no young lady should see," Father said.

"Don't kill them, Father," I said.

"Nobody will get killed," Father promised. "Unless they are very foolish."

When Father led the boys away, I was left with the dark, wind, and my confused thoughts. My mother was right, of course. I was twenty years old and not only still unmarried but even without a man to call my own. I had to settle down soon.

After years of drifting, my life had speeded up these last few days. First, there had been the militia with Ensign Hepburn, and then Niall had shown some interest. The interference of Eilidh added some tension to that friendship if it was nothing more than a friendship. As well as that, there was that dangerous Excise man Campbell and the surprisingly weak Mr Gillespie. I shook my head. I had promised to look in on Mr Gillespie from time to time. That had been three days ago. Unless Mr Gillespie had made a quick recovery, he would still be lying there in that cold room. He may even have died.

That was not a pleasant thought. I resolved to check the unfortunate landowner just as soon as I could.

"Fiona! Are you deaf?" I became aware that Father had been shouting for some moments. "Bring the garrons!"

Untying the hobbles, I led the first garron up the path, knowing that the others would follow. These Highland ponies were as sure-footed as any goat and would plod on forever, in any conditions.

"Look." Father stood at the peak of the pass, a massive figure against the pink dawn that flushed the eastern sky. I joined him and smiled.

The men of the glen had ambushed the militia, stripped them of their uniforms and tied them back to back in their underwear. Now they sat there amidst the heather, blindfolded so they could not recognise us and helpless as newborn babies.

You may think me a cruel, heartless woman, but I could not resist my smile. It was funny to see so many proud men sitting there, dressed in only their underwear when they had come to our glen to rob us of our livelihood.

Perhaps I should have felt sorry for them. I did not.

"They do not look gallant now, do they?" Father asked.

"They do not look like the soldiers who defeated Bonaparte's hordes," I said. "Or like the men who conquered Hindustan."

I ran my gaze over the men, wondering how they felt being defeated by what they would consider a bunch of Donalds, the term of contempt they used for Gaelic speaking Highlanders such as us. I started when I saw Ensign Hepburn at the end of the line. I had not thought that my freckled little friend might be among them.

Suddenly, I was not so comfortable with the sight. If Ensign Hepburn had led this picket of militia, I worried he might get into serious trouble from his commander, the hard-faced captain.

"What are you going to do with them?" I asked.

"I do not know," Father said. "I was thinking of throwing their muskets into the loch and leaving them here, tied up." He glanced at me. "I was not thinking of shooting them, Fiona."

"I am glad of that," I said. "It would be so untidy having a dozen dead bodies cluttering up the hillside."

I stood there in the flushing of the dawn with the unhappy

militiamen sitting on the damp heather and the wind increasing in force.

"They are not used to the hill weather," I said. "It would be a kindness to let them back to their barracks."

"You are too soft-hearted, Fiona," Father said.

"It is practical," I said. "If we are cruel to the soldier-boys, their captain will wish his revenge, and we already have Malcolm Campbell swearing blood and death upon the glen."

Father looked sideways at me. "You are not as foolish as you can sometimes look," he said, which was as near to praise as he could stretch.

"Hobble them," I said. "Tie their hands and attach *buarachs* to their legs so they cannot walk quickly and allow them their freedom."

"We can do that." Father was smiling. "Niall, take the boys home," he raised his voice. Fiona and I have things to do here."

Father had an almost unlimited ability to surprise me. I had not expected to be chosen to hobble the militiamen, and yet there I was, tying wrists together and attaching *buarachs* to their ankles with as much gentle efficiency as I could. Naturally, I chose my ensign and tied him up, wondering if he recognised me through his blindfold.

"You'd be better letting us go," Ensign Hepburn said as I pulled up the legs of his woollen underwear and tied the *buarach* around his slender ankles.

I said nothing. The poor boy was already shivering with cold. I felt like rubbing his back to bring warmth to him. Instead, I helped him to his feet and turned him to face the direction of his barracks.

"In a moment, I will remove the blindfold from one of you," Father deepened and roughened his voice. He also spoke in English so these intruders could understand. "You will walk there; you will not run. Twenty muskets are pointing at you, so if you turn around, we will shoot you flat and leave you to rot in the hillside. Do you understand?"

My poor ensign nodded his head so vigorously that I thought it would fall off.

"Go then," Father ordered and removed the ensign's blindfold.

Ensign Hepburn straightened his shoulders. "South Edinburgh Militia!" his voice was surprisingly strong. "We have met with a temporary setback, yet we are still soldiers. Slow march!"

"Well said," Father murmured his approval. "That young man has spirit."

I felt something like pride as Ensign Hepburn led his men in a stumbling walk down the pass, with each man trying to pick his way over the uneven ground, littered as it was with boulders, loose stones and patches of heather. I watched my ensign with his slim form encased in these white, tight underclothes and wondered what he was thinking as he took tiny steps. We must have sorely tried his pride.

"They will walk until they think we are no longer watching," Father said, "and then they will stop, take off their blindfolds and untie each other."

I heard one of the Militiamen yell as he stumbled and Ensign Hepburn gave encouraging words.

"Our boys are long gone now," I said. "I have an idea. At present, the militia must be burning with hatred for us."

"I would imagine so," Father agreed.

"What if they thought that one of us was friendly," I said. "Then we would have a spy in their camp."

"You are thinking of that ensign," Father said. "The fellow you spoke to when they first came into the glen."

"That is what I am thinking," I said. I was thinking a great deal more than that, although I did not wish to admit it. I had developed a small liking for Ensign Freckles, although he was evidently not a warrior.

"You also have a softness for him," Father surprised me by saying. "How will you cultivate this friendship?"

"I will help him by untying him before he does it himself," I said, "and by being sympathetic to his plight. After all, you have won this round; there is no denying that. Now I can give light to him and see if he opens up to me."

"You are a cunning woman." Father paid me a great compliment. "Off you go then before it is too late."

By now, it was full dawn, grey light was seeping into the glen between the gaps in the hills, bees were busy on the heather bells, and the cattle in the pastureland were demanding that I milk them. Glen nan Gall was looking at its best, and I was happy with life.

Lifting my skirt, I nearly skipped down the hillside to the front of the stumbling column of militiamen.

"Oh! Oh, Ensign Hepburn! What has happened to you?" I called out as if surprised and shocked at the same time. "Who has done this terrible thing?"

"Miss Gunn?" Ensign Hepburn looked embarrassed, as well he might when a young woman surprised him as he was walking about in his underclothes. He adopted that strange, awkward crouch that men do when they are trying to cover themselves. "What on earth are you doing here?"

"I saw you from the glen," I said, not entirely lying. "I wondered what you were. I thought you were a procession of ghosts, all in white and walking down the pass. What on earth happened to you?"

"We were ambushed," Ensign Hepburn said. "There must have been a hundred of them at least, and before we knew it, they overpowered us."

"At least a hundred and fifty," one of his men said. "All big men in tartan with guns and swords."

"I saw more than that," another of the militia stated, and I thought I'd better interrupt before they imagined another Jacobite Rising and called for the government to send up ten thousand regulars to put down the rebellion in the glen.

"I did not see a hundred men with guns," I said. "Now, if you could all stand still, I will have those silly blindfolds off you."

"Halt!" Ensign Hepburn commanded, and the slow stumble down the hill stopped.

One man promptly fell and lay on the ground. I walked along the column, gently removing the blindfolds that I had tied in place only a short time before.

"There now," I said. "Is that not better? You can enjoy this lovely morning."

"We'll kill them," one ungrateful militiaman said. "We'll march through the glen, shooting them flat!"

"All one hundred and fifty of them?" I asked. "Now turn around, and I'll release your hands. I have found one of the bayonets those hundred and fifty men stole, and I will cut you free."

The militiamen obliged, so I walked the length of the column, slicing through the heather rope. Some thanked me, others swore, some rubbed their wrists while the more intelligent immediately began to unfasten the hobbles around their ankles. Leaving them to sort themselves out, I concentrated on Ensign Hepburn. I unfastened his wrists with a little more care and then crouched at his feet to slice through his hobble.

"You look cold," I said. I could see that my ensign was shivering. "What happened to your nice uniforms?" To be honest, he looked quite fetching in his close-fitting woollen underwear. I did not tell him that I wished to hug him as if he was a pet dog or one of my younger brothers after Mother had taken him to task for some petty misdemeanour.

"The smugglers took them," Ensign Hepburn said, shamefaced.

"I gathered that." I tried to garner my patience, although I am not by nature a patient person. "Did you see what they did with them?"

"No," Ensign Hepburn said.

I swear that he was close to tears.

"They won't be far away," I said. "Shall we hunt for your uniforms? It would be better if you returned fully dressed." I allowed myself a small smile as I stepped back to survey him.

"Unless you desire to remain in that costume? It is rather sparse for this time of year, although interesting."

Ensign Hepburn did not seem amused at my attempt at humour. Men are strange things. They will laugh at the misfortunes of others while being utterly mortified when they are the butt of another's diversion.

"Where did these rogues attack you?" I hid my smile.

"At the head of the pass," Ensign Hepburn said.

"Come on, then. Doubtless, your uniforms will still be there, waiting for you in their loneliness."

We returned up the pass and poked around in the heather. I had expected Father to throw the uniforms into a peat hole, and so it proved. They were floating in the dark water, all arms and legs and with the brave scarlet now soiled and sodden.

"You cannot wear them in that state," I said truthfully. "You'll all catch your death of cold."

"What do you suggest?" Ensign Hepburn and his men were at a complete loss what to do out in the hills. God help us if the French ever invade; the country would need a woman to lead us. That young Victoria lassie might do; she seems a spunky piece. Anyway, the militiamen. stared at me, hopeful that I could find a solution for all their problems.

"We need a fire," I said, remembering that at least one of the militia had been smoking. "Has anybody a flint?"

One of the older men produced a flint, wet now after its immersion in water. I waved it in the air to take off the worst of the moisture and ordered them to gather dry heather stalks. They obeyed at once, and I had the entertaining sight of a dozen men in their underwear crawling about the heather at my command. Now that was an experience to relate to my grandchildren.

When my personal servants had gathered a pile of dried heather, I managed to scrape a spark and blow it into a tiny flame. Heather stalks burn well when they are dry, and within a few minutes, I had a respectable little fire going.

Ordering the boys to keep searching for fuel, I spread out their clothes, circulating them in front of the flames until they were sufficiently dry to wear.

All this time, Ensign Hepburn was watching, making little comments and giving bad advice, as men liked to do, and looking more and more like a lost puppy.

"It may be an idea to look for your muskets," I advised. "Your captain will be a bit miffed if you tell him you've lost them all."

"Oh, yes," Ensign Hepburn said and ordered some of his men to begin a search.

"Try the peat pools," I said. I knew how my father thought.

It was well into the forenoon before all my men were dressed in their finery again. I viewed them and smiled, quite proud that I had transformed a mob of near-naked men into something that looked reasonably military if not yet fit to fight the French. Or anybody else, unless they were very small and did not carry any weapons.

"Found them!" A young militiaman shouted, and within a few moments, the militia had their muskets back.

"Now," I said to Ensign Freckles. "What on earth were you doing up here in the dark anyway?"

"We knew that the smugglers were coming this way," Ensign Hepburn said. "We did not know that there would be so many of them."

He was sticking to his story about being ambushed by overpowering numbers. I thought that would amuse father.

"How did you know about the smugglers?" I asked.

Ensign Hepburn gave a smug smile that made me wonder about my previous liking for the boy. "Ah," he said. "We have another friend in the glen."

"Oh, indeed?" I professed admiration. "Does he have a name?"

"He is a she," Ensign Hepburn said. "And the most adorable creature you could ever hope to find."

There is a saying that you always pay for your good deeds, and that was how I felt. I had wasted half a morning helping this ungrateful Edinburgh buffoon, and here he was praising some other woman. I had to restrain my urge to slap his face as it had never been slapped before and then kick his shapely rump into the bargain.

"Oh," I said. "That's nice."

"Yes, the women in this glen are much friendlier than the men." Ensign Hepburn preened himself a little, perhaps thinking that he possessed some boyish charm that we "women of the glen" found irresistible.

"I wonder who she could be," I said truthfully, for I wished to catch the treasonous bitch and throw her headfirst into a peat hole and watch her legs kick as she drowned.

"Oh, that would be telling," the silly little boy tried to tease me.

"It's Mhairi," I said, drawing a name out of thin air. "She told me how handsome you were."

"No," Ensign Hepburn said. "Her name is not Mhairi."

"Don't lie to me." I smiled through my anger. "I know that woman. Anyway, it does not matter." I turned away, flicking my hair in the manner that always attracted the attention of the boys. "I know where some illicit whisky is hidden. I bet Mhairi could not tell you that." I stepped away, wondering if my ungrateful ensign would bite.

He did, grabbing at the bait like a trout on the end of the line.

Men are such simple creatures, I thought.

"You know where illicit whisky is? That would be a good result for my picket."

I smiled and said nothing.

Did this man think that his captain would forgive him for being ambushed and humiliated merely because he came back with a keg or two of peat reek?

"Tell me where, Fiona." Ensign Hepburn adopted a more

wheedling tone now as he begged me to do him a favour. There would be threats soon, I guessed.

"You do realise that withholding intelligence about an illegal action is against the law."

There was the first threat. I retaliated in kind.

"You do realise that withholding a rival girl's name from your sweetheart is against morality."

I waited for his reaction. First, he had to work out what I meant, and then he had to analyse how it affected him. I knew that could take some time with Ensign Freckles, so I looked away and hummed a little song.

"Sweetheart?" I was surprised that he fixed on the most important word. Ensign Hepburn was more intelligent than I had supposed.

"That was what I said." I continued to hum as we marched down the pass and into the glen. I knew that half the glensfolk would be watching us, standing outside their homes or in the fields, wondering what Calum Gunn's daughter was doing with the sojer-boys.

Well, at that moment, I was wondering that myself.

"Are we not sweethearts?" I injected a mixture of hurt and query into my voice. "Do you think I would have come to help a dozen near-naked men if anybody else except you had been leading them? I may have ruined my reputation, and now you tell me that Mhairi has already taken my place in your affections."

Good God, I could spout the most awful drivel when I had to, *could I not*? But that's how we spoke. We lived with our hearts on our sleeves, read romantic poetry and shielded our hate for the landowners who were destroying our culture with so-called Improvements.

"Oh, Miss Gunn." Ensign Hepburn stared at me for so long that he missed seeing a hummock of heather and sprawled all his length.

I helped him up while his undisciplined men guffawed and nudged each other in the ribs. Oh, how I wished that I could have command of them for a week or so. I would've taught them respect."

"Up you get, Ensign Hepburn," I said, helping the clumsy oaf to his feet.

"I must have tripped," he said.

"That is what happened," I kept my voice grave. "That heather is treacherous at times. Now, you were telling me about Mhairi."

"I was not," Ensign Hepburn said. "I was asking why you said sweetheart."

"Because we are," I told him, flicking my hair again. "I would not be here else. Do you think I would have helped you all if that captain what's-his-name had been in charge? It was only for you, Ensign Hepburn." I laid it on as thickly as I could. "Only for you."

He looked at me. "The woman who helped is not my sweetheart," he said at length.

"I am sure Mhairi will not be pleased to hear that." I stopped then. "Do you see that group of rowan trees?" I indicated a small copse that grew beside a lochan. They were in full fruit with the red berries ablaze in the glen.

"Yes," the ensign caught on. "Is that where the whisky is hidden?"

"Ask Mhairi," I suggested. I was growing rather bored with this game now and wondered if I should just run home. None of these militiamen could catch me across the glen, and I mighteven lure them into a peat bog. However, I was wild to find out the name of our informer, so I decided to continue.

"Don't you trust me?" I changed tack and dangled temptation before him. "Would you trust me if I found you a keg of peat reek?" I took a step further away from him.

"I would be pleased," Ensign Hepburn said.

"In that case, follow me. I can do better than Mhairi, who evidently alerted the smugglers to your presence."

"It was not Mhairi!" Ensign Hepburn said.

"Oh, for goodness sake," one of the older soldiers said. He had the twin stripes of a corporal on his arm. "Her name was Eilidh. Now can we get back to the fort?"

"Of course," I dropped in a curtsey to the corporal. "Ensign," I said. "There is a keg of whisky beneath these trees." I ran off before he could reply.

I knew the paths across the moor and how to avoid the peat-bogs. If any of these lumbering Edinburgh folk tried to follow me, I wished them the best of luck. I had sufficient of their company for one morning and, more importantly, I had discovered the name of the informer.

7

"Eilidh Mackay!" Mother shook her head. "Now, what would make that little madam run to tell the soldiers about us?"

"A pair of tight breeches," Father said, crudely, "and what they contain."

"That's enough of that kind of talk," Mother snapped. "There are children in the house."

"I am sure they know all about it." Father winked at me, and I could not restrain my smile.

"That is no reason to encourage them," Mother said. "Well, now, we will have to do something about Miss Eilidh."

"What do you suggest?" Father asked.

"I think we should drown her in a peat bog," I said helpfully, thinking of the blonde beauty upside down with her dress around her waist and her legs kicking madly. It was rather a favourite vision of mine, and I savoured it for the next few minutes as Father pondered my idea and Mother gave a *tchah* of disapproval.

"I mean," Mother said when Father's roar of approval died down. "Shall we tell people or use her to spread false information?"

"I rather liked the drowning idea," Father said and sighed. "Your plan is more subtle, though. I knew there was a reason why I married you."

With a house crammed with children, I could think of another reason but thought it best not to comment. Instead, I nodded. Mother was the best possible foil for Father. While Father did all the practical work, distilled the spirits and organised the delivery, Mother had control of the purse strings and the house and planned the future. She was the brains of the business.

"All right then." Mother pursed her lips and pressed her fingers together to form a little pyramid. "I will think how best to use Miss Eilidh. Calum, you have to find another market. Malcolm Campbell will have all his resources to close off Perth to us now. Think of Dundee or Aberdeen."

Father nodded; he was sensible enough to follow Mother's advice.

"Fiona, how friendly are you with this ensign?" Mother asked.

I shook my head. "I like him, Mother, but he is very immature. He has cute freckles and a pleasant smile, but he is not marriage material, if that is what you mean."

"That is not what I mean," Mother said. "You will not marry a soldier. I want you to be very friendly to him and find out all you can. You are our Eilidh."

"Yes, Mother." I nodded. When Mother gave orders, we obeyed.

"Good. Keep out of this soldier's bed. I don't want any accidental grandchildren." Mother's look would have bored through granite.

"Yes, Mother," I said again.

"Good. Now, what about that other fellow."

"Who? Niall?" I looked up in puzzlement.

"No, the landowner chap."

"Oh, dear God! I forgot all about him!" I covered my mouth with my hand. "I left him all alone with a damaged ankle. He may even be dead by now."

"I hope not. I charge you with his safekeeping, Fiona. Go to him now and look after him. With Malcolm Campbell hunting us, we will need all the help we can get, and you are our best hope. Go now!" Mother pushed me to the door. "And for heaven's sake, girl, don't let him die!"

"Yes, Mother," I said. "I just need to collect a few things."

Bees were busy in the tangled shambles that had once been a garden around the Big House, and I gathered an apron full of brambles from one of the many bushes that acted as a barrier to any intruder foolish enough to try to break in.

"Mr Gillespie!" I pushed open the door. "Mr Gillespie, are you in here?"

"Here," the voice was little more than a croak.

He lay precisely as I had left him on the roll of bedding in that dismal room. The fire had gone out days ago, leaving only a tiny pile of ashes and the charred end of a stick.

"Are you still lying here?" I asked in genuine surprise. Any male in my family would have forced himself up, however ill he felt. My father had never had a day's illness in his life, while my brothers ignored minor cuts and bruises and fretted whenever my mother ordered them to stay indoors.

"I can't move," Mr Gillespie said.

I shook my head. "Well, Mr Gillespie, in that case, you will need my help." I kept my voice cheerful even though I was a little tired of mothering a grown man who apparently was made of weaker fibre than the youngest member of my family. "Have you eaten?"

He shook his head. "Not since I finished what you left."

"You've not shaved either," I said, running my hand over his stubbled jaw. "Come on then, let's get you sorted out."

I made up the fire first. The house was large and had been empty for years, so there was no hardship in finding rotted floorboards and such like rubbish. I happily ripped the place to shreds and took piles of timber through to Mr Gillespie's room.

"You'll feel better when you're warmer," I said. "Then we'll get some food in you."

With the fire sparking brightly in the grate, I fetched water from the well and heated it up.

"I'd better wash and shave you," I said. "Do you have a razor?"

"Yes," Mr Gillespie said shortly. "I can wash and shave myself."

"Then why didn't you?" I said, more tartly than I had intended. Mother wished me to be kind to this useless man, so I forced a smile. "Well, that doesn't matter. Once you've done that, I'll have a look at your ankle and ribs, and then we'll eat."

"I've nothing in the house," Mr Gillespie said.

"I've brought some bannocks," I told him. "And a couple of trout from the loch, with a skelp of cheese."

Mr Gillespie looked interested. "Where did you get all that?" he asked.

"My mother's house," I said. "Except for the trout. I guddled them on the way over."

"You what?"

"Guddled them. I put my hands in the water, and when the fish swam into them, I hauled them out." I did not tell him that it was poaching. He was the landowner, so legally, they were his damned fish anyway.

"I always thought people caught fish with nets or lines." Mr Gillespie looked at me sideways. "What other tricks do have up your sleeve, Miss Gunn?'

"Och, Mr Gillespie, there are as many ways of taking a fish as there are of skinning a cat. You can burn the water with a lantern, or use a snicker, that's a treble hook with a lead weight on top, or you can tow an otter, that's a board armed with a score of hooks." I paused, wondering if I had said too much. Mr Gillespie seemed interested. "There are more, none of which matter at the moment. Is your throat sore?" I knew it was by his hoarse voice. "I can make up something for that."

"What would that be?" He was already washed and had scraped the stubble from his face with a razor from his bundle.

"Whisky, honey, and hot water," I said.

"We have the hot water, but no whisky and honey," Mr Gillespie croaked to me.

"Give me twenty minutes," I said. "In the meantime, eat this." I handed over a bannock and the brambles I had collected from his garden. "The fruit will make it sweeter."

I split and gutted the trout and placed them on a flat stone on top of the fire. "These fish will cook while I am out," I said. "Now, don't you dare move."

I had heard the bees when I entered the house, so tracing them to their hive was the act of a minute. Wrapping my shawl around my face and head as protection, I robbed the hive of a slice of honeycomb and withdrew, ignoring the angry buzzing as the bees defended their home. I considered the two stings on my arm as well worth the price.

"Fresh honey," I said and smiled. "My favourite food." That was true, even then, I had a sweet tooth. I could have eaten fruit and honey all day and every day, while the occasional, and very expensive, cup of chocolate that the peddlers brought tasted like a piece of heaven.

"You've been stung," Mr Gillespie noticed.

"It's nothing," I said truthfully as I poured hot water into the pewter mug I found in his bundle and spooned in a generous amount of honey.

"It's a pity there is no whisky," Mr Gillespie croaked.

"Oh, but there is." I showed him the leather bladder that I had carried from home. "The best ferintosh in Scotland."

"You are a resourceful woman," Mr Gillespie said. "You can produce food, drink, and medicine from the air."

"Glen nan Gall provides for us all," I said. "If we could only grow chocolate here, the world would be complete."

Mr Gillespie smiled. "I don't think the climate would allow

for that." He sipped at his mug. "What do you call this concoction?"

"A hot toddy," I said. "If I had more time to spare, I would brew you something to prevent the onset of sore throats."

Mr Gillespie raised his eyebrows. "And how would you do that?"

"Bramble juice, honey, vinegar, whisky, and hot water," I said. "I don't know how it works, but it does. It tastes vile, but if you take it at the first onset of a cough, it fights the disease."

"I will bear that in mind." Mr Gillespie took a deep draught. "I feel better already."

I eyed him as he lay at his leisure in the mess he called a bed. "Right, Mr Gillespie," I said. "You've lain there for days doing nothing. It is time you tried to move a little, or your ankle will forget what it is meant to do."

"I can't move." He looked up at me through big eyes, much as my younger brothers did when I told them it was time to learn to write.

"Your ankle is a lot better," I adopted my stern voice. Honestly, men and children are much the same. It takes a combination of kindness and strictness to manage them. "Up you come. I will help you."

I suspect he did not expect me to be strong enough to lift him, but the women of the glen are used to physical labour. We cut and carry peat and herd animals along with the men, and outdoor work is. Living in the Highlands does not make for a race of insipid weaklings.

He balanced on one leg, half-smiling as he leaned on me. "What now?"

I could smell the honey and whisky on his breath and see a small patch of stubble that he had missed on his chin. That made him more appealing. It was hard to believe that this helpless man was the owner of Glen nan Gall.

"Now we try to walk outside," I said. "You need fresh air and the smell of the hills. This damp indoors is no good for you."

"The fire will dry it up," Mr Gillespie said.

"It will dry it up whether we are in or out," I told him, severely, "and better for you to be outside. Come on."

We limped out of the door together, and he looked along the dark corridor. "I don't know this house," he said. "Perhaps I should explore it first?"

"Fresh air is better." I stuck to my guns, although it may have been more diplomatic if I had followed my landlord's wishes. "A few minutes of clean air will have you feeling a lot healthier. Come on."

I guided him out of the side door. The bees were still lively, the brambles as black and juicy as ever, and the sun had decided to peep through grey clouds, gladdening us with a caress that was nonetheless welcome for being only lukewarm.

"Glen nan Gall," I said. "Your land now."

I stopped to allow Mr Gillespie to survey his property. He nodded, looking around. "It is as I was told," he said.

"Who told you about the glen?" I asked. "I know that you are not from these parts."

"It is in my family," Mr Gillespie said. "My people came from here."

"Oh?" That interested me. "So you are a local man? I don't know the name, Gillespie." Many people ended up in the Glen of the Strangers— refugees from defeated armies, stragglers from victorious armies, women running from abusive husbands, gaberlunzies who decided to hang up their pack, the waifs and strays of history washed up on our boggy land and remained here. We were a stubborn bunch with no connection to clan or country. Our loyalty was only to the glen.

"My people were. I have never been here before." Mr Gillespie took a deep breath of the mountain air, coughed, and then tried again.

I watched, knowing that fresh hill air was a sovereign remedy for most ills. It would either cure him or kill him.

"Welcome home," I said, wondering if Mr Gillespie would fit

in with my people or if he would be a bird-of-passage as so many of those before him. "Do you intend to live here, or will you live elsewhere and use Mr Snodgrass as a Factor?"

"What is the standard practice?" Mr Gillespie asked.

"It was once normal for clan chiefs to live among their folk," I said. "Now, that is less likely to be the case. They are clearing the people from the land and using it for sheep farming or sporting estates." I could not stop the bitterness from entering my voice. "Some have sold their land to outsiders who do not know or understand the country and its people. To them, it is a place for sport or profit. The old relationships between people and chief are gone, they cannot listen to the whisper of the wind or speak to the hills. They are alien, they do not belong here and never will."

I realised that I might be saying too much and clamped shut my mouth. Mr Gillespie was the new landowner. He might've had plans to clear the glen of people and bring in the great white sheep to destroy the land or even use Glen nan Gall as a hunting estate as was happening to so many glens in the Highlands.

Callous, greedy landowners had evicted thousands of their tenants, creating wildernesses from once heavily populated glens. The rich wished to shoot deer and live in an environment he considered romantic and natural. What was natural about a place that once rang with children's laughter of children being empty except for the shriek of the wind and the bang of a hunter's? These sporting landlords are selfish, spoiled, useless, vicious creatures. They are a blight on the land, an infestation on Scotland, and I put my curse on them and all their type.

"I have heard the stories," my reserved Mr Gillespie said. "Tell me about this glen of yours."

"It is not my glen," I said. "It is yours. You have bought it and signed the papers."

"I still cannot believe that," Mr Gillespie said. "I own all this land, and on my first visit, my tenants attack me." He shook his head. "Are they asking to be evicted?"

"They did not know you were the landowner," I said, trying to apologise for my father. "They thought that you were the gauger, the Exciseman."

Mr Gillespie faced me with his eyes as intense as anything I had ever seen in my life. "A community cannot exist on illicit distilling," he said. "Sooner or later, the law will catch up with them."

"There is nothing else," I felt very uncomfortable to have the truth put in such a direct fashion. "The cattle trade is depressed, there is no industry, and the glen barely has enough soil to grow crops. We have had a string of absentee landlords, years of them, ever since the White Lady." I stopped there, not wishing to say more.

"You were paying rent when I first met you," Mr Gillespie said. "To whom?"

"To the Factor," I said. "Mr Snodgrass runs the glen even when there is no landowner."

"Does he indeed?" Mr Gillespie nodded. "I shall investigate the business of Mr Snodgrass. Who was the previous owner?"

"An English gentleman," I said. "He came once and did not return."

"Perhaps not surprising if the locals gave him the same reception that they gave me."

I smiled, remembering the previous landowner. "He arrived in November when the rain was hard, took one look at the big house and did not return. The glen was up for sale a few days later." I returned his scrutiny. I knew that he had the power to evict us all, yet we were of the glen and would not be cowed.

We were of the old beliefs in our glen and knew we must *dree our weird*– endure our fate– God was in charge, and whatever He had chosen, then that was what would happen. We would not complain. I also knew that my father had his methods of enduring, and if any landowner evicted us, that landowner would not have had a pleasant future.

"And the previous landowners?" Mr Gillespie's expression gave little away.

I shrugged. "They came, they saw, they left. Some did not come at all, one stayed at the King's House, the Inn, but none lasted."

"Not since the White Lady," Mr Gillespie said softly.

"Exactly so," I could see where he was going. That was fine. I could go there as well and let Mr Gillespie make of it as he would.

"Tell me about her," Mr Gillespie asked softly.

"You may need to sit down," I said, casting my eye around the jungle that was once a garden. There was an old iron seat here somewhere, hidden among the tangle of brambles and rampant weeds. I cleared a path for my invalid and led him to it. He sat without demur and looked around.

The glen was at its peak with the heather purple under a soft sun, the hills rounded and watchful, and the burns a silver-white streak as they scored the flanks of the braes. If there is a paradise, then it must be modelled on a Highland glen, or at least a Highland glen before the savage cleansing of the Improvers.

I knew Glen nan Gall best, but at one time, all the glens would've been like mine. There were fields fertilised by the hardy black cattle, clachans of heather-thatched cottages, golden crops in the long-strip fields, peat cuttings for fuel and potatoes in lazy beds. I savoured the scene, enjoying the laughter of women and children as everybody worked in God's pure air.

"This is your glen," I said softly. "It is beautiful."

Mr Gillespie did not smile. "Tell me about this White Lady," he said.

"As you wish." I brushed away a couple of questing bees. "They won't sting us if we leave them alone," I said. "But all the same, I don't wish to swallow one."

Mr Gillespie nodded. "The White Lady," he insisted.

"Her name was Cummings," I said and then paused. That

name was bitter in my mouth, as it was in the mouth of every person in the glen. "Isabell Cummings, and she fell heir to the glen in her youth. People say that she was the most beautiful woman ever to grace the Highlands, so blonde that her hair was nearly white and so perfect of figure that even the cattle in the fields stopped grazing to watch her pass."

"Isabell Cummings sounds like some lady," Mr Gillespie said.

"Indeed," I agreed. "Isabell Cummings came from a long line of Cummings who had owned the glen for generations. The name was once Comyn, but they changed it— that is another story. They were not often here, for they had extensive lands elsewhere, in the low country of Moray as well as throughout Badenoch and even as far as Lochaber in the west and the Garioch in the east." I paused, trying to bring the words into my mouth while all the time the hatred was building.

Gaels can store hatred like no other, you see. We smile and talkand behave as we are supposed to yet, underneath, we are hating and waiting, and one day it will all come out, and there will be revenge. It may take a year or a decade or two centuries, passed from generation to generation, but it is there, coiled like a snake. Woe to those who have wronged us on that day, and the landowners of the Clearances and the men and women who force us from our land will regret they ever heard the name of Scotland.

"When was this?"

"Oh, quite recently," I said, "only twenty or thirty years ago. Isabell Cummings dressed in white and rode a white horse. She was indeed the White Lady. Every year she demanded the people of the glen hunt pine martens so she could make coats for her friends."

"Was that instead of rent?" Mr Gillespie asked.

"No," I said. "That was as well as rent." I let Mr Gillespie think about that for a minute before I continued. "Even so, Isabell Cummings did not believe that people paid her the respect that she was due. She saw that the establishment held others in high regard, others such as the Duchess of Gordon and Lady Sutherland, and she wished to be spoken of in the same breath as they were."

"Was she a titled lady?" Mr Gillespie asked.

"She was not," I said. "She was the owner of Glen nan Gall and is that not sufficient honour for anybody, man, woman, or monster?"

Mr Gillespie nodded. "I understand your point."

"Isabell Cummings did not understand that point. She watched Lady Sutherland and the Duchess of Gordon and learned what they did that made them so valued. The White Lady lived at the time of the Great French War, you understand. Napoleon Bonaparte threatened invasion, and every man and his dog were in the Fencibles or the Volunteers or the Militia. All the young lads hoped to prove their courage against the French. Isabell Cummings saw that the Duchess of Gordon had raised a regiment of Gordon Highlanders and Lady Sutherland had the Sutherland Highlanders, and she wanted the same."

"Sound the trumpets, beat the drum," Mr Gillespie said quietly. "Cesar and Uranius come." He shook his head. "Purcell and his kind have a lot to answer for."

"Oh? Who is he?"

"Purcell was an eighteenth-century composer," Mr Gillespie said. "He is one of the men who glorify war.

Bid the Muses haste to greet 'em,
Bid the Graces fly to meet 'em
With laurel and myrtle to welcome them home."

Mr Gillespie looked at me and coloured briefly. "Sorry, Miss Gunn, I have interrupted your tale."

"That's quite all right, Mr Gillespie," I was unused to hearing men quote poetry. The nearest equivalent was the roaring out of some Gaelic song or the retelling of Ossian or another epic.

"Pray continue," Mr Gillespie said.

"Isabell Cummings decided she too would raise a regiment. She called it The Badenoch Highlanders, and sent her Factor to

Glen nan Gall to spread the bad news. Naturally, the men were reluctant, for it was one thing to join the Volunteers who would defend the glen or Scotland, but quite another to be a regular soldier. Eventually, the White Lady came in person, astride her white horse, and backed by the Factor, Mr Snodgrass's father, the Lord Lieutenant and a man in a scarlet uniform and with fancy feathers in his hat who was to be the colonel of the regiment. He was a red-faced fellow."

"What happened?" Gillespie was listening intently.

"The White Lady called an assembly at the Stone of the Gathering, where men used to muster for war many centuries ago. She told the glen that she was building a regiment to fight for freedom. Unless all our young men joined, she would evict their parents and burn the thatch above their heads so they could not return."

I imagined the scene as I sat on that cold iron seat with the bees busy around us and the clouds drifting around the slopes of Am Bodach.

"That was her idea of freedom?" Mr Gillespie asked.

"That was her idea of freedom," I said.

"How many joined?"

"The men mustered, grumbling, angry but knowing that if they did not, then their mothers and fathers and sisters would be out in the cold, like Clan MacIain of Glencoe in the old days." As I told the story, I was pushing my own plans, of course, for I wished this landowner to see how unfair it had been for the folk of the glen. I was trying to turn him to our point of view.

"You are still angry about it all these years later," Mr Gillespie said.

"Years do not alter facts, and an evil is an evil," I said, rather more hotly than I had intended.

"Carry on," Mr Gillespie invited.

"The men gathered as I said, and the Colonel, whose name I forget, marched them out of the glen and up the Bealach nan

Bo," I pointed out the gap between Am Bodach and An Cailleach. "Up there."

"I see it," Mr Gillespie said. For a moment, we looked upwards, where mist smeared the hills and closed the pass in a smudge of grey.

"They were marched south for half a day and then halted for the night. And those same hours of darkness, there was a killing in the glen. The White Lady was found dead, her body stripped to the skin and left at the summit of the pass as a warning to all landowners that the glensfolk could retaliate when they suited." I paused, allowing my words to sink in.

"Who did it?" Mr Gillespie asked the question that a succession of landowners had asked for nearly thirty years.

I shrugged. "Somebody must know," I said. "Without the White Lady, there was nobody to raise the regiment, and the men all returned home, save for a handful who decided that adventure beckoned more strongly than the lure of hearth and family. We did not hear of them again."

"What happened to them?" Mr Gillespie asked.

"I do not know. As I said, we did not hear of them again. Not a single one of these soldiers returned to Glen nan Gall. Perhaps they died in Spain under Wellington, or in Egypt, or India. I do not know. History and the great French war swallowed them without a trace."

"That was thought-provoking," Mr Gillespie stood up, balancing on his right foot. "I wondered why the glen was so inexpensive compared to others. Now I know."

I helped him stand. "Landowners tend to come and go quickly or to walk wide of us, knowing the history," I said. "I hope it has not put you off."

"Not at all," Mr Gillespie said. "I have plans for this glen." His smile was rare but worth the wait.

I felt something cold clutch at me. "I hope you are not going to clear the people," I said.

"I am not," Mr Gillespie told me. "And I am not going to be

an absentee landlord either. Now, how well do you know the Big House?"

"Not well at all," I said.

"Then we can explore it together," Mr Gillespie said. "If that is all right with you? Am I keeping you from your work?"

"I am happy to explore the house with you," I said. I did not tell him about the mission that Mother had found for me. I hauled out a fallen branch and trimmed it with Mr Gillespie's knife. "Use this as a walking stick," I said.

"I prefer the support I have," he said, and I knew that he meant me.

"As you wish," I said, wishing that Niall or Ensign Hepburn had been so forward.

8

I had not intended this friendship to happen. I allowed myself no feelings for Mr Gillespie. I had some liking for Niall, who had grown on me during our trip to Perth. I rather liked Ensign Hepburn, although he was hardly the heroic type and would not last a week living in the glen without his soldiers to support him. Mr Gillespie was a bit of a weakling to give in to a sore ankle. I did not wish any entanglement with a man who took to his bed at the slightest excuse. Besides, he was a landowner and would probably not remain in the area for longer than a few weeks, despite his fancy words.

"Then that is the support I shall give you," I said lightly, hoping that he wanted no more than my arm for a prop.

If he thought he was going to inveigle me into his bed on the strength of him owning the glen, then he was wrong. I was my father's daughter in many ways and would fetch Mr Gillespie such a clout as would land him on his back. If he were lucky, I would only break his other ankle. If he were unlucky, then I would severely damage a much more delicate part of his anatomy. Having a clutch of brothers gave me experience in such matters.

"Have you never been inside the house?" Mr Gillespie asked me.

"Not until I took you here," I said. "Nobody has been inside it since three days after the White Lady died."

"Why three days?" Mr Gillespie asked.

"The Cummings family removed the possessions," I said. "They locked the door, and nobody has been in since." I did not say that we enjoyed watching the big house crumble slowly to the ground.

"I understand." Mr Gillespie said. "Well, we are here now, so let us explore it together."

The ground floor was a wreck. Most of the windows were broken or had frames that had slipped out of place. The floorboards were riddled with rot and dampness, while cobwebs hung grey and thick across ceilings and in every corner.

The rooms were larger than I had ever seen, yet they were not homely. I preferred the crowding and conviviality of my home.

There were two flights of steps to the first floor. One flight was wide and wooden, with an ornate bannister that only needed some elbow grease to polish it to something beautiful. The second was much narrower, with rough stone walls without any pretence at decoration.

"That must be the servants' way up," Mr Gillespie said. "We will take the grand staircase."

With our footsteps echoing in the dark chamber of a hallway, and the only light seeping through filthy windows, we tested each step and found them surprisingly sound.

"I wonder what is up here." Mr Gillespie leaned heavily on me, and I wondered if he was tiring or merely wished to hold my arm. I thought of Niall and Ensign Freckles and wished either of them were in place of Mr Gillespie.

High, multi-paned windows allowed more light to the upper storey, and Mr Gillespie stopped at the landing.

"This looks promising," he said.

I agreed.

There was a wooden-floored corridor, off which half a dozen doors opened. We walked along, examining each room as we came to it. The first room was vast, with a magnificent plastered ceiling and a chandelier that had miraculously survived the passage of years with no more damage than a covering of cobwebs. Oak wainscoting covered the lower part of the walls, and a wall press offered scope for further examination.

"Might I look?" I asked, suddenly curious about this mansion that had lain undisturbed for so many years.

"Of course," Mr Gillespie said. "I would race you if I had two sound legs."

We both laughed at that small sally, which surprised me. I had not expected humour from a landowner. I was first to the wall press and tugged open the door. When it refused to move, I tried again, nearly falling as it opened with a jerk, and Mr Gillespie put an arm around me.

"Careful there," he said in that rich, slow voice that was beginning to intrigue me.

"Thank you." His arm was warm and surprisingly strong for a man who gave in so readily to a hurt ankle. "What do we have in here?"

There was some cutlery in the press, bits and pieces of china, and a teapot that may have been silver. I was not sure, having no experience of such material.

"Good quality," Mr Gillespie lifted the teapot, rubbed off the surface dirt and tapped the front. "Do you recognise that coat of arms?"

I looked carefully, spat on the teapot in a most unladylike manner, and then rubbed again. The eagle was unmistakable. "That is the symbol that is above the front door," I said.

Mr Gillespie nodded. Taking back the teapot, he turned it upside down. "See that tiny mark there?" He pointed to a couple of symbols on the bottom. "That proves that it is real silver and was made in Edinburgh."

"Oh." I took the teapot from him. "I've never held anything made of silver before."

"Do you like it?"

"It could be beautiful if you cleaned it up a bit." I handed it back.

Mr Gillespie shook his head. "Keep it," he said. "It's yours."

"But it's real silver," I said. "And you—" I hesitated for a second. "You need every penny you have."

Mr Gillespie raised his eyebrows. "Do you think so?"

"Well," I said, "if you don't mind me saying so, I think you spent all you have when purchasing the glen. You don't live in luxury, do you?"

"No," Mr Gillespie smiled. "I don't, do I? I had better get my plans for the glen started soon then, don't you think?"

I was not sure what to say to that. "What are your plans?" That was all that I could manage.

"I plan to make it work," Mr Gillespie said, "and make it profitable. Keep the teapot. You have more than earned it with all you have done to help me."

"Are you sure?" I held it tightly. "Nobody has ever given me anything before."

"I'm sure." Mr Gillespie was smiling. "It's only a teapot. You deserve a lot more."

"Thank you," I said. "It will look good in our house."

"Good. Now, let's see what else we can find." Mr Gillespie smiled. "We might find a pot of gold or a chest of jewels."

I smiled back, enjoying this side of Mr Gillespie. "Or perhaps a chest of tea for the teapot." Mr Gillespie was not aware that tea was very much a luxury item in the glen.

The next room was smaller and plainer, with green painted shutters on the window and a crib lying on its side in the centre of the floor.

"This must have been a nursery once." Mr Gillespie lifted the crib to an upright position. "Do you have any children?"

"Me?" I squawked. "Good God, no! I am not married."

"No, of course not," Mr Gillespie said. "How silly of me."

"Are you married, Mr Gillespie?" I do not know why I asked that question.

"I am not," Mr Gillespie said. He looked around the room again. "Let's see what else we can find."

I felt quite light-hearted as we entered the next room, which was identical to the last except without the crib. A small, plain door connected the pair. "The nurse's room," Mr Gillespie said.

After another two rooms that could have been used for anything, Mr Gillespie opened the final door on that floor.

"Now, this is worth seeing," he said as he entered. He still limped heavily and held onto the wall for support.

I stepped in behind him. This room was by far the largest on the floor, with three large multi-paned windows overlooking the hills to the south and garnering the best of the light. The fireplace was decorated in classical plasterwork, and the cornice was a copy of an Adam masterpiece although, at the time, I had never heard of the man.

In the centre of the ceiling, surrounded by a yard-wide rose, another chandelier hung. Time had been unkind, with many of the crystal pendants detached. Some lay on the wooden floor under a film of dust, while others winked on the only piece of furniture in the room, the largest bed I had ever seen.

"A four-poster!" Mr Gillespie exclaimed. "That will be more comfortable than my shake-down on the floor."

I stared at the bed in awe. I had never seen anything quite like it before. Four carved pillars soared to within a few feet of the very high ceiling, with the bed at least nine feet long and five feet wide.

"This must be the master bedroom," Mr Gillespie said. "I will bring my wife in here someday."

I nodded. "Do you intend to live in this house?"

"I have known about this glen all my life," Mr Gillespie said. "I dreamt about coming here, and I dreamed of owning it. Now

I do. I dreamt about living here with my wife and bringing up a family."

"Does your intended wife know your plans?" I wondered if he had even told his fiancé about Glen nan Gall. Certainly, there had been no women visiting the glen since Mr Gillespie had arrived.

Mr Gillespie smiled at me. "Oh yes," he said. "She was the first person I told."

"Oh," I did not understand my sudden swoop of disappointment. "I think you had better clean your house up a little before she comes."

Mr Gillespie gave a secretive little smile. "I will move into this room tonight," he said. He pressed down on the bed. "The mattress will have to go. It will harbour every little crawling creature known to man."

I agreed, although I had a secret desire to see whatever infested that mattress attack Mr Gillespie and his wife as they lay together on that bed.

I recalled the reason that I was here. Mother had given me a job to do. "I'll help," I said. "The straw in the mattress will burn well, and fire will rid you of any unwanted guests." I looked around the room. "This place could be pretty if somebody cleaned it up." Suddenly keen to see what could be done, I grinned at Mr Gillespie. "Come on then, Mr Gillespie. Let's get on with it."

"What, now?"

"Now," I said. "We'll need brooms and a fire."

It was the work of five minutes to carry a lighted branch from downstairs, and by that time, Mr Gillespie had pulled the mattress from the bed, coughing in the choking clouds of dust. He proved adept with his knife, ripped open the mattress, and hauled out the contents, which we found to be more dust than straw.

"I'll keep the fire alive," Mr Gillespie sounded happier than I had ever known him.

"You're making more mess than ever," I said. I was busy making a heather broom, tying bunches of heather together.

I picked up all the fallen pieces of the chandelier, placed them carefully inside my new teapot for safekeeping and set to work. I had to stand on the bed and stretch up to reach the high ceiling and laughed when Mr Gillespie complained about being showered with dust and pieces of cobweb.

"It serves you right," I said, "for letting your house get into such a mess!" I knew that joking with the landowner was perhaps not a sensible thing to do. I also knew that he grinned at me through his film of dust and cobwebs as he fed the contents of the mattress into the fire.

I continued the dusting, scouring that room with amazing energy. It took an hour to burn the mattress, and at one point, the soot and accumulated rubbish in the lum— the flue— caught fire. We listened to the roaring, held each other, and hoped that we had not set the whole house up.

We had not, although the descent of great lumps of glowing soot was somewhat disconcerting. We laughed at our fear and continued to work. By the time we burned the mattress, the heat had chased away all thoughts of dampness in that room.

Now, it may have been a strange way to spend a day, but I had my motives, and getting into favour with Mr Gillespie was only one of them. I did not understand the others' reasons or the terrible aftermath of that most confusing of days.

"You have done a good job here," Mr Gillespie said when we had completed the dusting and the cobwebs and their attendant spiders banished from the room.

"I have only started," I told him, rolling up my sleeves. "Before I am finished, this room will be fit for a queen or the Lord of the Isles."

Mr Gillespie smiled. "What do you plan next?"

"Keep that fire burning," I said. "I am going to give these windows the wash of their lives and scrub this floor as nobody has ever scrubbed it before!"

Heather is a most versatile plant and the rougher stalks make an excellent scrubbing brush if correctly cut. All I needed was Mr Gillespie's knife and a few strands of cord which the roots of heather also supplied. With hot water and energy, I soon altered the colour of the floor from grey to a marvellous pine yellow, and once I had washed the windows inside and out, the room looked bright and cheerful.

"I can't believe the transformation." Mr Gillespie had been sitting on the bed, watching.

"Up!" I ordered, with no thought at all for his position or wealth. "You've sat there long enough doing nothing. "I want this bed polished, so it is fit for a human, not a dog."

Mr Gillespie stared at me as if I had insulted him. "What?"

"Up!" I repeated, dragging him from his lazy perch. It was instinct and long habit that made me slap his bottom, as I did with my brothers and sisters when they shirked work. "Come on now. Get to work."

For a moment, I wondered how he would react. Perhaps I had gone too far? I stepped back, half expecting him to lash out at me or throw me out of his house. He did neither.

Mr Gillespie's laugh echoed around the room. "You are a queer little creature, to be sure," he said. "One minute you are a princess among nurses, then you are the queen of housewives, and now you are bullying me." He shook his head.

Once I had started, I knew I had to continue. I could not back down. "Well," I said. "Come on then, Mr Gillespie." I passed over a handful of heather stalks. "Get that bed cleaned."

"Yes, miss," Mr Gillespie said and, kneeling on the ground, he worked to my instructions.

I watched him, and I don't know quite how I felt. I only know that I had never ordered a landowner around before and probably never would again. Yet, it did not feel unnatural. I had seen him grimacing in pain. I had washed the blood and mud from his face. I had tucked him up in bed and heard him snore. I had fed and watered him and knew that he was only a man. He was nothing more and nothing less.

With two of us working and only one piece of furniture, we had that room fit for royalty in no time.

I stepped back, looked around and nodded. "That will do," I said. "Now, I will not feel sorry for you lying on your bed of rags."

Mr Gillespie got off his knees. "You have made quite a difference," he said.

"*We* have made quite a difference," I corrected him. "All we have to do is transfer your bed and belongings up here, and you will feel more at home." I gave him a sideways look. "Although I suspect that your sweetheart will expect a few more creature comforts than a bed frame and a fireplace."

"Oh no," Mr Gillespie said. "She is the most admirable woman. She will adapt to every circumstance imaginable."

"I am sure she is a very worthy woman." I decided to say no more about Mr Gillespie's sweetheart.

Let him find out himself what a refined lady thought about living in a single room with only one piece of suggestive furniture and not even a curtain across the window. I tried to picture this unfortunate lady, seeing her with her piled-up hair and her silk-and-satin dress tripping across the wet heather. I am sure I gave a most unpleasant smile.

Mr Gillespie had a great deal to learn. I did not know then that I would meet his sweetheart sooner than I expected, and the revelation would shock me.

"Wait," I said and handed over the fallen pieces of his chandelier. "You will need to attach them again." I watched as he stood on the bed and stretched upwards to fit them. Each sliver of crystal had its own tiny hook, and Mr Gillespie's large hands struggled with the intricacies, so I had to join him. We stood together, side by side on that massive bed, working the delicate little pieces of glass until the chandelier, dusted and complete, was as pretty as anything I had ever seen.

We stepped to the floor together, with Mr Gillespie stumbling as his bad ankle gave way. I caught him by instinct, and we smiled at each other.

"Thank you," Mr Gillespie said.

"It's about time that ankle healed," I told him. "If it's not better in a couple of days, I will take you to see Doctor Fraser in Aberlour."

"Oh no," he said. "It will be all right by then."

I hid my smile. On the odd occasions that the boys in our family were sick, Mother always threatened them with the doctor. That always created a miraculous recovery. Males do not seem to like visiting doctors, which always amused me greatly.

"I am glad to hear it," I said solemnly.

After the work and fun on the second floor, the top storey was a bit of a disappointment. There were five rooms, all smaller than those on the floor below and none worth comment. Empty of furniture, they were dusty and dark, with dampness creeping in from the damaged roof above. There was nothing to salvage and nothing much to see.

"You'd best get home now," Mr Gillespie said.

I nodded, yet there was sadness within me as I walked back to Penrioch. I had enjoyed those hours in the big house and hoped that the lady of the house appreciated the work that I had done. I knew that she would not. The landed class only cares for things that increase their wealth. Ordinary people such as me do not count for anything in their self-centred lives. As I pondered, I wondered how Mr Gillespie regarded me. He probably saw me as an upstart tenant with a long nose, useful for hard work and nursing him when he was sick. Such thoughts put me in a bad mood as I returned home.

My mother listened to my news, nodding at all the correct places. Together we wondered about Mr Gillespie's lady.

"She will be some stuck up Edinburgh creature," Caitlin gave her opinion, and I agreed with feeling.

"They are all the same," I said, consigning Mr Gillespie and all other landowners to the same hot place. I did not know, then, what had put me in such a foul mood after a day of laughter and cheerful work.

Mother watched me. "I will have to see this Mr Gillespie." She touched my shoulder. "You did a good job today, Fiona. Now forget him for a while. You are right to think that the so-called upper classes are all the same."

9

"A stranger woman is staying at the King's House." Grainne, the youngest and prettiest of my sisters, brought the news, and the word soon spread around the glen. In a community such as ours, any new happening or event spurred our interest. When we were not discussing Old Man Hector's latest illness and wondering when he was going to die, we were criticising Donnie Mackay's cattle or wondering how the Shaw's grew such weed-free barley.

"What sort of stranger woman?" I asked, with my head full of Mr Gillespie and his lady.

"I don't know," Grainne said crossly. "I heard that there is a stranger woman at the Inn. Is that not news enough for one day?"

"You did well to come and tell us," Mother soothed over the burgeoning argument, casting a hard look at me. I had been in a black mood ever since I returned from the House of the Eagles, and I was spoiling for a quarrel with Grainne. "Did you hear anything else about this lady, Grainne?"

"No, Mother." Grainne gave me a look of smug triumph. I fought my desire to slap her hard. "If you wish, I shall ask Seana

Grant. It was Seana who told me, and she got the news from her brother Niall."

"You go and do that, please, Grianne," Mother said. "And Fiona will find Niall and ask him." Her look convinced me that arguing was not an option. "It will do you good to meet Niall again, Fiona."

I sighed to show my displeasure, threw down the potatoes I had been washing as further proof, muttered that I would complete my task later, and then stomped away.

"Be nice to him, mind," Mother called after me. "He may be your future husband."

"My future husband," I repeated savagely as soon as I was out of my mother's hearing. "As if I would settle for a man such as Niall Grant."

I knew Mother was correct. I knew that a man such as Niall Grant was what I would settle for, and unless I were quick, I would be lucky to land him. What was the old saying that I have already quoted? *Men chase women until the women catch them.* Niall was certainly not the type of man to do any chasing— except if he had his eyes on Eilidh, the informer.

Although the Excisemen could only find one still hidden around the glen, the glensfolk knew where they were. We had nine other stills, all complete with an eighteen-gallon capacity still, with three casks to hold the distilled spirits. There was a short worm, the copper coil that was hard to obtain and harder to replace, and a wooden tub and a stillhead.

At this time of year, with the barley harvest nearly completed, there were worts ready for distillation and a camouflaged roof over everything. In our glen, with the Allt Gobhlach burn running fresh from the loch and a score of small tributaries, there was never a shortage of sweet water.

Niall was working a still deep within a peat bog, with the faint smoke hidden by the mist across the surface of the water. He looked up when I approached.

"Hello, Fiona. I thought you would be with your militia friends."

"Not today," I sensed the tension in his voice. "Young Grainne tells me you saw a visitor at the Inn."

Niall nodded. "Yes, some south country woman." He smiled. "She did not appear impressed with the lodging. I heard her whining voice long before I saw her."

I did not care about the complaints of some unknown woman. "Who was she?"

Niall shrugged. "I don't know. I never asked." When he smiled, he did look quite handsome. He stood up. "Why do you want to know?"

"I wondered if it was Mr Gillespie's sweetheart," I told him honestly. "He mentioned he had a fiancé. I want to see the woman who will have great influence over the glen."

"Run down to the Inn if you wish," Niall said. He looked up. "Or maybe just look along the glen. Here she comes now, and with a friend, no less."

"What?" I looked up.

"Stand here." Niall indicated a small knoll in the middle of the bog. "You can hide behind that stand of heather." He grinned. "That's where I stand when the Excisemen come to the glen."

I stood where Niall had suggested. The slight rise gave a surprisingly extensive view from the opening of the glen all the way to the Big House and to the road that led to Dunbeiste. I looked in that direction, wondering about Ensign Freckles.

"Try this." Niall produced a small spyglass.

"I did not know you had one of these." I allowed him to hold my arms as he demonstrated how it worked with the sliding tube and the different lenses.

The first woman leapt into focus, appearing so close that I nearly let go of the spyglass in astonishment. Tall and elegant, she stared straight ahead and controlled her white mare with no apparent effort.

"She is lovely," I said without thought, for she was indeed attractive.

"Oh?" Niall showed some slight interest. "Let me see."

"Wait a minute." I waved him away. "I want to see the other one as well."

The second woman was a few years younger and rode a few yards behind her companion. She was looking around, holding her hat with her left hand and guiding her horse, a black-and-white mare, with her right. There was something vaguely familiar about her, although I knew I had never seen her before in my life.

"Let me see." Niall's impatience got the better of him as he grabbed the spyglass from me and peered at the women. "The tall one's not bad, I suppose," he said. "If you like women who ride with their noses stuck in the air."

I smiled, wondering if Niall was saying that for my benefit or if he was serious.

"If she has ridden the entire distance from Edinburgh like that," Niall continued, "she must have a cast-iron backside." He winked at me. "Either that or it's more cushioned than it looks."

"Niall Grant!" I admonished him in pretended shock. "You are rude."

I had to admit that Niall was correct. The tall lady, whoever she was, rode side-saddle and so erect that she was nearly leaning backwards. "I must go closer," I said, handing back the spyglass.

Such is the nature of our glen that the track winds past the fields and patches of bogland, while a woman or man on foot can cut the bends and run far quicker, so long as she or he knows the safest routes. I arrived at my favourite watching spot a good three minutes before the ladies rode up and perched myself on the wall. I waved as they approached.

"Halloa!" I called.

The leading lady favoured me with a single glance and looked away without a word.

"Halloa!" I shouted again. "It's a lovely day."

"Isn't it beautiful?" The second rider smiled, still with one hand holding her hat. "Are you a local lady here?"

"I am from the glen," I said. "Are you lost?"

"Lost?" The second rider laughed. "God bless you, no. My brother is an officer at the fort here."

"Oh," I said. "That's nice." It was bad enough that the militia should infest our glen without bringing in their relatives as well. That is the worst of South Country folk. One will come and appear friendly, and then another, and before you know it, they are buying up the place and pushing us out of the land our ancestors have lived in for centuries.

"Perhaps you know him?" The smiling lady reined up beside me. Try as I might, I could not dislike her.

"Captain Barrow? I have seen him in the distance," I said.

"Oh, bless you, not the gallant captain. My brother is much less exalted. Ensign Andrew Hepburn."

I very nearly said, "Ensign Freckles," but had sufficient sense to curb my tongue. "Yes," I said. "I know him." That was the familiarity I had noted. Ensign Hepburn shared some of the same characteristics as his sister.

"Do you?" The lady was every bit as impulsive as her brother as she smiled at me. "Are we on the correct road to Dunbeiste?"

"It is straight ahead," I said. "That old fort at the foot of the pass."

"Thank you." The lady said. "And the mansion house? Is that nearby as well?"

"The mansion?" I wondered at the name. *Dear God! Ensign Freckles' sister must be Mr Gillespie's intended!* "Oh yes, but we just call it the Big House."

The lady laughed. "The Big House! How lovely."

"It's not in great condition." I was about to ask the lady if she was Mr Gillespie's fiancée when she spoke again.

"You don't happen to know a girl called Pistol, do you? It's a queer name, I grant you."

"Pistol?" I shook my head. "There is nobody in Glen nan Gall by that name," I said.

"That's what Andrew calls her. Little Pistol."

"Little Pistol." I knew that Ensign Hepburn was referring to me. "Does the Ensign have any regard for the mysterious Little Pistol?"

"Andrew has the highest regard for her." The lady lowered her voice, no doubt scared that the watching cattle may carry her tale, or perhaps she was afraid there might be fairies hidden among the heather.

I smiled. "If ever I meet this lady, should I tell her that she has a secret admirer?"

"Oh, do come along, Amelia!" The leading lady's cross voice floated towards us. "I don't have the time to spend with the natives, and quite frankly, nor do I have the inclination."

"That's me," my cheerful lady said. "I am Amelia Hepburn." She waved and raised her head. "I'm coming, Charlotte!" About to push on her horse, she smiled again. "I am awful! I did not even ask your name."

"I am Fiona Gunn," I said.

"Amelia!" Charlotte's voice was sharp.

"I have to go," Amelia said. "Thank you for your help." She gave a small wave as she trotted after Charlotte, leaving me to ponder what she had said.

Little Pistol eh? I would take Mr Ensign Freckles to task over that when next we met. Little Pistol. I admit my lack of height, and I supposed that changing Gunn into pistol might have been mildly amusing to an infantile mind. Despite my attempt to be miffed, I smiled. I was quite pleased that my ensign had spoken of me, even although not quite in the manner I would have wished.

10

"Well then?" Niall asked. "Who were they, and what did they want?"

"One was Amelia Hepburn, Ensign Hepburn's sister," I said. "And the other was Charlotte something-or-other. I did not get her last name. She was the stuck-up one."

Niall nodded. "Aye, if we are lucky, she'll fall into a peat bog or a patch of nettles."

I said nothing, enjoying my mental vision of the arrogant Miss Charlotte face down in a peaty puddle or sitting in a bed of nettles. Yes, I thought. Yes, I would like to see her in either situation.

"The Hepburn one was friendlier. I think she is Mr Gillespie's intended."

"More important than that," Niall said, "these two women may distract the militia. Your father has arranged another cargo of whisky this Friday, and with that damned Exciseman sniffing around, things could get sticky."

"I haven't seen Campbell these past few days," I said.

"Nor have I," Niall said. "And that worries me. If I can see the Exciseman, I know what he's doing. When I can't see him, I think he's up to mischief."

"Father knows what he's doing," I said.

"Your Father knows what he's doing," Niall said, "but he also likes to twist the lion's tail. One of these days, he's going to go one step too far, and the lion will turn around and bite him."

"I hope that day does not happen," I said.

※

MOTHER NODDED WHEN I TOLD HER ABOUT THE TWO WOMEN as we made bread together on the table.

"You think that this Amelia Hepburn is Mr Gillespie's girl, then?"

"She was asking about the Big House," I said.

"That makes some sense," Mother frowned. "I wondered about the sudden appearance of the army and Malcolm Campbell at the same time as we have a new landowner." She shook her head. "I don't think your crippled Mr Gillespie is as innocent as he makes out."

"I think you are right, Mother," I agreed. "He seems to be hand in glove with the militia."

I now regretted helping the helpless Mr Gillespie as much as I had. I hoped that his chandelier fell on him as he lay on his fancy bed. It would've been even better if it fell on him and the amiable Miss Hepburn as they lay together.

"Well then, it's best to find these things out." Mother said. "We may have a surprise visit from Campbell and his friends." She tested the dough, nodded, and told me to place it on the fire. "When that happens, I wish you to keep quiet and not get involved. Do you understand?"

"Yes, Mother."

"Good." Mother nodded. "It will not be easy."

11

It did not take long before Campbell's Excisemen were infesting our glen.

"Here come the gaugers." Father stood at the cottage door as the autumn dawn rose angry and red above the hills.

Malcolm Campbell led the unit, sitting tall on his saddle, and with four Riding Officers behind him. As befitted a scion of Satan, Campbell wore all black, with a high-crowned beaver hat on his head and his coat flapping around him as he rode up the glen.

"We could shoot them all flat," Niall said quietly.

"And bring more trouble on ourselves," Mother said. "Best stand back and watch them. "Do you have anything incriminating inside your house?"

Niall shook his head. "Nobody has," he said. "Your husband has made sure of that. The clachan is clear as new-made spirits."

We watched as the gaugers splashed through the puddles and passed the infields where we had recently cut the first of the barley.

"They're not even coming to the clachan," I said.

"No," Father said. "They're heading for the alder trees." He swore. "I've a quarter anker buried there."

Mother and I exchanged glances but said nothing. I knew Mother was thinking the same as I was: Eilidh Mackay knew too much.

The alder trees grew in an untidy clump beside a small half-hidden burn. Campbell led the Excisemen straight to the spot and snapped an order that saw them dismount and probe the ground with their long, metal-tipped staffs.

"Aye," Father said. "They know what they are doing."

"Campbell must have been spying on us," Niall said.

"That is possible," Father balled his fist. "We can remove the gaugers, as Niall suggested."

"No." Mother put a hand on his sleeve. "That is not the way, Calum. If Campbell and his men disappear, others will come in their place. Until now, the militia has been ineffective. If there are murders in the glen, Mr Gillespie will have to call in the army, and things will get much worse."

"I can have my pistol in two minutes," Niall said.

"Wait, Niall." I put my hand on his arm, rather enjoying the hard swell of muscle I felt there. "Perhaps the gaugers will not get things all their own way all the time."

Niall glanced at me and then Mother. "You two have something planned," he said.

We did not reply. We watched as the gaugers probed the soft ground around the base of the alder trees. One man shouted in triumph, and the others gathered around. Taking small spades from their horses, they dug down and produced a quarter anker keg.

Father said an ugly word.

Without delay, Campbell placed the keg on the back of his horse and mounted up. The others followed.

"Now where?" Niall asked.

"They're going to the lochside," Mother said.

Producing his spyglass, Niall watched the progress of the Excisemen and reported to us. "They're stopping at the old clachan of Auchiemore," he said.

"I've a keg hidden there," Father said.

"Campbell has a paper in his hand," Niall reported, "and he is giving out directions to the others. They are digging on the side between the ruins and the loch." Auchiemore had been vacant for twenty years. It had been the home of one of the few men who had joined the army. He had not returned, and when his parents died, nobody had re-occupied their home.

"That is where I buried my keg," Father said.

"They have it," Niall reported.

We watched all morning as the gaugers headed straight for the location of the whisky, unearthing keg after keg as they toured the glen. Father said little as he saw his profit and the livelihood of his family diminish seizure by seizure.

"I hope they are feeling proud of themselves," Father said, "sending a family into poverty and starvation over the winter."

"They have no concern for families," Mother said. "They think of government revenue and the bounty money they make for each seizure."

I could feel the despair of defeat settling on me. It was noon before Campbell and his men stopped their searching.

"They're coming here," Niall said.

"Let them come," Father sounded grim. "I have something within the house that will welcome them with lead and fire."

"No, Calum." Once more, Mother placed a restraining hand on his arm. "Let things take their course."

The gaugers rode straight for us, with Campbell in the lead and the kegs bouncing in panniers on their horses' flanks. We waited for them, wordless.

"You have been watching us." Campbell reined in at our side.

"We have," Father said.

"You will know that we have found a large number of kegs of whisky." Campbell could not keep the triumph from his voice. "We will be back for the stills."

"I wish you joy of your searching," Father said.

Campbell snorted. "As soon as I can put evidence on you, it will be the prison or a hefty fine."

"I am sure you know how to plant false evidence," Father said.

Campbell smiled. "In this glen, there is no need for such measures." He leaned closer to Father. "This is a glen of smugglers, cattle stealers, idlers, and immorality."

"There is no immorality in Glen nan Gall," Mother replied. "Only the cruelty and oppression that will disappear the moment the tail of your horse vanishes from our glen."

Campbell laughed. "Oh, you think I am cruel and oppressive, Madam? Then I congratulate you on your ignorance."

"Good bye, Mr Campbell." Mother flicked her skirt aside as if the gauger's very presence contaminated her.

"Good bye, Mrs Gunn. I would advise you to get used to life without Calum. I will ensure that he spends a long time locked up."

Touching a hand to the brim of his hat, Campbell kicked in his heels and walked his horse away. The Riding Officers followed, some eyeing us, others leering, and one middle-aged man avoiding our eyes as if in shame.

"They're not leaving the glen yet," Father said.

"How much did they get?" I asked.

"About a quarter of my supply," Father sounded disconsolate.

"Good," Mother said. "That leaves you with three-quarters, which is plenty. It has also proved to Campbell that his spy is to be trusted."

"Mother!" I stared at her. "I thought you had already spoken to her."

"Not yet," Mother's smile lacked any mirth. "Come with me, Fiona, we have work to do."

"So have we," Father said to Niall. "Come on Niall, we have whisky to make."

Eilidh was busy at her spinning wheel when Mother and I called at her family home. "Hello, Mrs Mackay," Mother said. "We're just here for a blether. God bless the work, Eilidh."

"And God bless the house and all in it," I added through gritted teeth.

"Did you hear what happened?" Mother asked Jean Mackay, Eilidh's mother and a decent, hard-working woman who deserved a better daughter, in my opinion.

"That was terrible yesterday with Malcolm Campbell," Jean Mackay shook her head. "Will Calum be able to cope with the loss of so much peat reek?"

"Oh, yes," Mother said, pitching her voice to ensure that Eilidh could hear above the whirr and clatter of the spinning. "Calum will be grand. After all, it's only the excess whisky. He has the stills in working order and producing steadily."

Jean smiled. "I am glad to hear that. I wonder how the gaugers got their intelligence about the hiding places."

I heard a slight falter in Eilidh's spinning.

"I saw a man on Am Bodach a few weeks ago," I said. "I think Campbell or one of his men has been spying on us."

"Oh, the dirty devil!" Mrs Mackay said. "Did you hear that, Eilidh? That Malcolm Campbell fellow has been up on the hillside spying on us."

"Has he?" Eilidh tried her best to look shocked. "That's awful." She threw me a look that could have melted cheese. "It's nearly as terrible as stealing another girl's man."

"All is fair in love and war." I met her glare with one of my own. Having so many siblings has made me quite an expert in the glaring department.

"He is my man." Eilidh dropped all pretence of working and stood up to face me. She overtopped me by a good two inches, so I had to tip my head back to meet her gaze.

"I think we should allow him to decide that, don't you?" I said. To be honest, I was still not sure that I wanted Niall, but I had no intention of allowing the blonde and busty Eilidh to get her claws in him. If the alternative were a lifetime of marriage to a man I did not love, well then, I would pay that price. It would have been worth it merely to parade Niall past Eilidh at every opportunity, and when I fell pregnant with his children, I would pat my belly and smile smugly. "Niall put that there," I would say, and enjoy Eilidh's discomfiture.

"Enough, now, sweetheart," Mrs Mackay said as my mother dragged me back.

"We're not here to fight with Eilidh," Mother reminded me that we had quite another purpose for our visit.

"Yes, Mother." I backed away, still looking daggers.

"Now apologise to Mrs Mackay for ruining the peace of her house," Mother ordered and, swallowing my pride, I did so, as Eilidh gloated.

"That's better," Mother said. "As I was saying, Mrs Mackay, Calum lost some of his whisky, but the stills are in operation, so things are not as bad as they could be."

Mrs Mackay smiled. "I am glad," she said. She was a smiling, peaceful lady who would not interfere in anybody's business.

"Father has moved much of the distilling to a new site at Toldhu," I said helpfully.

"Mrs Mackay does not wish to hear their locations," Mother said.

We both hoped that Eilidh had been listening.

"It's all right Mrs Gunn. I won't tell anybody," Mrs Mackay said.

"I know you won't," Mother agreed. "I just don't think it is fair to burden you with knowledge that could be dangerous if the gaugers hear. Imagine if Malcolm Campbell learned about the Toldhu still." Mother shook her head. "That would put half our operation out of business. Young Niall Grant would have to find work outside our family as well."

Nicely said, Mother, I thought. *Use Niall as a lever to further persuade Eilidh to inform on us.*

"As long as that devil Campbell has not seen it," I added, "we should be all right."

With the business part of our visit completed, we moved onto other topics, such as the oncoming winter, the declining health of old Hector Shaw and all the comings and goings in the glen over the past few weeks.

"I don't know," Mrs Mackay said. "There are many strangers in the glen, with the militia at Dunbeiste and the new landowner in the Big House. Now there are these two South Country women. I honestly don't know what the world is coming to."

"Our Fiona spoke to the women." Mother seemed proud of my bravery. "Didn't you, Fiona?"

"Yes, Mother," I said dutifully. "They were Amelia Hepburn and Charlotte somebody-or-other. Amelia seems a jolly sort of girl. She is sister to Ensign Hepburn of the militia, and I think she is the new landowner's intended."

"Oh, is she?" Mrs Mackay was ready to absorb this juicy titbit of gossip. "I can't imagine the soldiers with sisters and mothers. They look so efficient and stern all the time, don't you think?"

"Yes, Mrs Mackay," I agreed, thinking that the last time I saw Ensign Hepburn, he was in his drawers, white and shivering with his bottom all stained with peat where he had been sitting. The memory was so vivid that it made me smile.

"What about the other woman? Charlotte?" Eilidh swallowed her pride to ask the question.

"Oh, we don't know who she was," Mother spoke on my behalf. "She was a stuck-up creature with a snooty attitude."

I could feel Eilidh's eyes boring into my back.

"We'll watch out for her then," Mrs Mackay said. "It sounds like she is somebody to avoid."

I nodded. "That would probably be best," I agreed.

"Oh, Mrs Mackay," Mother said. "Fiona has had a marvellous gift from the new landowner."

"Indeed?" Mrs Mackay said. "What is that, pray?"

I listened in some discomfort as Mother told Mrs Mackay

about our silver teapot. From there, the conversation drifted again to poor Old Man Hector, who was rapidly declining in health and the new minister, who seemed a weakly fellow from the Lowlands.

※

FATHER HAD ARRANGED FOR A WARNING SYSTEM AT THE approaches to the glen, with women hanging out three items of white linen when Campbell and his gaugers were coming. The show of white in the glen alerted us the following week when Father was tanning leather. He called us all into action as the Excisemen rode up the glen.

"He's coming in force this time," Father said as we hurried to Toldhu.

The name means the Black Hole, and that is what it was, a black peat bog amid a dip, with a lochan in the middle and a low-lying island half-visible.

"You know what to do," Father said.

Niall and I exchanged glances. I was nervous after the previous disaster.

"It'll be all right," Niall said, while Catriona, wild as the heather and always ready to have fun at anybody's expense, laughed and tossed her hair.

"Let them come," Catriona said, and I imagined her whistling up the caterans for a raid on the Low Country or leading a force of MacRaes to join the Bruce or Donald Dhu MacDonald. She was that kind of girl, my friend Catriona.

We made ourselves look busy as the gaugers rode down the glen, with Father lighting a small fire in the pretence of distilling. To an outsider, it would appear as if we were making peat reek, with the scurry of activity and the haze of smoke around the loch.

"Halloa!" That was Campbell's voice, hard-edged and unpleasant. "Calum Gunn!"

Father looked up as though surprised to see the Excisemen standing at the side of the bog. "Oh, it's yourself, Mr Campbell."

There were six Riding Officers with Campbell and two men I guessed to be Sheriff Officers or their type. The latter were thick-set, muscular fellows with low-crowned hats and ugly bulges under their arms where they hid blackjacks or pistols. They looked like men well used to trouble. At least the Riding Officers, the soldiers of the Excise, carried their cutlasses and firearms in the open. They were honest enough rogues, after a fashion.

"*Bha sigh fad an so,*" Campbell said. "You have been long here."

"Indeed," Father shouted. "Do you intend paddling to come to me?"

"Show me the way," Campbell ordered. "In the name of the king!"

"And does the king require my directions to cross a bog in his own kingdom?"

As the Excisemen watched in uncertainty, Campbell dismounted and stepped onto the bogPeat-bogs can be dangerous places, with sucking mud that can drown a man, or they can be mere muddy areas where the wet peat barely reaches your ankles.

"Take a step to your right," Father said, "and three paces forward."

Campbell stopped, with peat-hags on either side of him. "And why should I trust your instructions, Gunn?"

"You asked for them," Father reminded. "You can do as I say, or you can flounder up to your neck in mud." He shrugged. "I don't care either way."

After a moment's hesitation, Campbell followed Father's advice and reached the edge of the loch with only muddy boots. His followers watched, either awaiting orders or unsure of themselves in our glen.

"How did you cross?"

We watched him from our island.

"There is a small boat here." Father indicated a coracle that lay a few yards from us.

"You are under arrest!" Campbell shouted.

"For what?" Father sounded bemused. "All I am doing is standing on an island in a loch. Here." He pushed the boat with his foot, so it bobbed into the lochan.

A lochan is only a small loch, often little bigger than a pond. Some can be extremely deep, with a peaty bottom that sucks in anyone foolish enough to try and cross. Others are so shallow that a child could paddle across and keep her knees dry. Not being a local man, Campbell did not know if it was safe for him to wade, and no man with sense would put a horse into a dangerous position.

Whatever accusations we can level at the Riding Officers, I had never known one to be deliberately cruel to his mount, while the Sheriff Officers, were townsmen, not prone to taking chances in this unfamiliar environment. Campbell looked at the coracle for a long moment while we watched and enjoyed his discomfort.

Father placed his hands on his hips and smiled. "Well, Mr Exciseman?"

"Don't try and escape," Campbell said and stepped into the coracle.

A coracle is a small, one-man craft made of cow-hide stretched over a wicker-work frame. It is not the most stable of boats and takes skill to manoeuvre across even a small area of water. I watched, hoping that the Exciseman would spin it around or, even better, topple himself head-first into the loch. Unfortunately, he did neither. He paddled across to us with some aplomb and landed on the island within a few strokes.

"Well, Gunn," he stepped onto the island. "Now I have you."

"And I have you also," Father said evenly. "What are you looking for?"

"I am looking for your still," Campbell said. "I have intelligence that you are operating a black bothy on this island."

"Search if you wish," Father invited. "You won't find anything." He stepped back. "We'll leave you to it."

"You'll stay where you are," Campbell said.

Ignoring the Exciseman, Father casually lifted the paddle of the coracle and stepped into the loch. The water only came up to his ankles, and we followed, being careful to place our feet exactly where Father did, for there was a crooked causeway that jinked this way and that across the lochan. Many Highland lochs have such pathways, relics of the long-gone days when people built islands on the lochs on which to live.

"Hold them!" Campbell roared as he realised we were getting away. The Riding Officers and Sheriff Officers tried to circle the lochan to catch us, but not knowing the secret paths, they soon became stuck.

Leaving the lochan, we followed Father across the bog, leaping from firm ground to firm ground and from rock to raised tuft of heather until we reached the edge. Once there, Father stopped and looked backwards. Campbell continued to scour the island for a non-existent whisky still while his men were floundering in the bog, some up to their waists in mud and others trying to help them out. One foolish fellow had attempted to ride across, and his horse was up to its withers and panicking. *Poor beast.*

"Good," Father said with satisfaction. "That will keep them occupied for hours. There is nothing on that island except a small fire and a fishing line."

I nodded. "Eilidh won't be so easily trusted next time."

"Campbell is watching us through his spyglass," Niall warned.

"I hoped he would do that," Father said. "Let's give him something to watch. Fiona, I want you and Catriona to leap over the heather in that direction," he pointed to the west. "Attract their attention and be visible."

"How do we do that, Mr Gunn?" Catriona asked.

"How do you get a boy to look at you?" Father was smiling.

"I roll my eyes and toss my hair, like so." Catriona demonstrated, much to Niall's consternation. "And then I walk away and swing my hips," she said and again caught Niall's eyes.

I nudged Niall sharply in the ribs. "You are looking too hard," I said.

Catriona laughed. "See how effective it is, Calum?"

"I see," Father said. "Now, that is fine when the boys are close. What do you do when they are further away?"

"Oh, in that case," Catriona said, "I would roll up my skirt as if I was trampling in the wash-tub." She lifted her skirt to mid-thigh, and Niall's eyes nearly popped from his head. I pulled him away from such ocular temptations.

"That's the way," Father approved. "Fiona, you join Catriona. Make sure that the gaugers see you."

"Why, Father?" I asked.

"Because Malcolm Campbell is no fool. Once he sees you two prancing around flashing your legs, he will realise that you are only a distraction, and he will concentrate on Niall and me."

"Yes, Father." I could understand that Campbell would expect a smuggler to use such a ruse.

"Well, Niall and I will be at the Clach-nan-chat." Father's face was a picture of innocence.

"Why?" I asked, although I already guessed Father's ruse.

"We will hide our still there," Father said. "Or rather, we will appear to hide our still here."

"Father!" I said. "You know what is at the Clach-nan-chat."

"I know what I am doing," Father said. "Now go and do what I told you."

"Come on, Fiona!" Catriona was giggling already, relishing the part she had to play. Looking over her shoulder, she saw the gaugers still stuck in the bog, with Campbell holding a telescope to his eye as he watched us move further away.

"They're watching us," Catriona said and waved. Lifting her skirt above her ankles, she ran up a knoll, with her feet twinkling through the heather. She laughed as she unfastened her hairband and allowed her auburn hair to cascade around her shoulders.

"Boys always like to see my hair flow," she said. "You do the same, Fiona."

"I am not as handsome as you are," I said.

"Many boys like a woman of your shape and size," Catriona scolded me lightly. "Boys don't all like the same thing, just as we don't all like the same type of boy. Why, Fiona, you have a fancy for Niall and also for that young Ensign, and they are nothing alike."

I stared at her. "I do not!" I denied, so hotly that Catriona laughed. I had not realised that my liking for Ensign Freckles was public knowledge.

"Yes, you do. I can see it every time you are with Niall. Your eyes brighten, and you lean towards him, and then you went to Dunbeiste to see that Ensign boy." Catriona laughed again. "I know such things, Fiona."

We reached the top of the knoll, where a shaft of sunlight penetrated the clouds and highlighted a rock of white quartz. "This will do, Fiona. Come on. Follow my lead!"

Somewhere in the moor, a whaup gave its tremulous call, the warbling sound melancholic as it raised the hairs on my head. Some of the old folk said that the whaup, or the curlew, was the devil's bird because of its long, down-curving beak, but I loved the sound it made and always stopped to listen. It was my favourite bird and cheered me.

"The whaup is calling for me," I said.

Catriona understood at once. She was empathetic, like so many Gaelic women of my time. That is a gift, or a curse, that we are e losing amidst the bustle of the towns. The world is all the worse for the loss. "I heard it," Catriona said. "Come on now, the boys are watching us."

Catriona posed at the top of the rock, thrusting out her left hip for the benefit of the gaugers. As they watched, she slowly lifted her skirt higher and higher until it was above her knee.

"Are they watching?"

"They are," I said.

Most of the Excisemen had stopped trying to wade through the peat and were staring at Catriona as she stood with her skirt up.

"Is Campbell also watching?"

"He is," I said.

"Join me," Catriona said. "You know what your father is after."

Taking a deep breath, for I was unused to such antics, I joined her. We both stood on that rounded rock with the sun warming us and the heather of the glen stretching as far as the out-fields around Penrioch and up to the dark heather-heights around.

"They're still watching." I felt very nervous with the men's eyes on me.

"Show your legs," Catriona said. "No, not quickly. Raise your skirt slowly, let the boys savour and anticipate."

Catriona was a born flirt. I was not, and I dragged up my skirt clumsily, stopping at my knees. I could almost feel the Excisemen staring at me. I looked sideways to see what Father was doing. He was approaching Clach-nan-chat, the Stone of the Cat, with some bundle he had lifted from a hidden hole in the heather.

"Come on, Fiona!" Catriona lifted her skirt higher, so the smooth skin of her thighs was exposed. I could see the white faces of the Excisemen staring at us from their entrapment in the bog.

Despite the distance between me and the gaugers, I felt the blood rush to my face as I copied Catriona. No man outside the family had ever seen my legs, and now I was displaying them to half a dozen strangers and that terrible Malcolm Campbell.

"We've got them trapped." Catriona was laughing. "They can't tear their eyes away from us."

I hazarded a look at Campbell. He had his spyglass extended, and then, as I looked, he moved the direction of his gaze to follow Father.

"It's working!" Catriona said. "Campbell has fallen for your father's plan." Her laugh was full of glee. "Right then, Fiona, let's give these boys something to see. Let's give them something to remember us by."

"What?"

"Follow my lead!" Catriona gave me the biggest grin imaginable, turned her back on the gaugers, and then lifted her skirt up to her waist.

"Catriona!" I gasped, scandalised as she bent forward and smacked herself across the bare rump.

"Come on, Fiona!" Taking hold of my sleeve, Catriona turned me around. "Show these gaugers what we think of them."

There was something strangely liberating in doing as Catriona asked, in lifting my skirt, so the cool air caressed my nether regions and in bending forward. Let the men see what they liked, I thought and gasped as Catriona smacked me with more vigour than I cared for. Her laugh was high and carefree, and then she stood up, jumped from the white rock, and ran across the heather.

After my previous protestations, I found myself hesitating a little. I knew that I would never find myself in such a position again, so I lingered slightly longer, gave a little wriggle of my hips to drive the image home and joined Catriona in running away. As an expression of contempt for the Excisemen, those few moments would've been hard to beat.

"Come on, Fiona!"

I will never forget Catriona's face as she turned ane held out her hand to me, so we ran together, laughing in freedom and friendship. It is a memory I treasure and one I needed to counter the black days that were to come. Damn you, Malcolm Campbell, and damn you, Mr Gillespie, for the troubles you caused me.

Father was waiting for us at a small group of rowan trees.

"Now watch." He took Niall's spyglass. "This could take some time."

After spending an hour in his fruitless search of the island, Campbell sat in the coracle and paddled by hand back to the bog. Careless of the depth, he rushed through the moss land, falling into three peat holes on his way, so he was encased in mud up to his waist and beyond long before he reached dry ground. Even from half a mile away, we could sense his foul mood as he shouted at his men.

"You girls did well," Father said. "Although I wouldn't tell your mothers what you've been up to." He gave me a twisted smile.

"Oh, my mother would quite approve," Catriona said. "She taught me all of that and much more." She leaned against me and whispered. "I will show you the tricks soon, Fiona. You might need them."

"It was quite a show." Niall grinned at me, then at Father and closed his mouth with a snap.

"There he goes," Father said, "straight for Clach-nan-chat."

With his bedraggled Excisemen at his back, Campbell arrived at the Rock of the Cat. Without hesitation, he took his metal-tipped stick and jabbed it underneath the huge rock. A second later, Campbell jumped back in alarm as a wildcat leapt at him, all fur and fury. Father laughed as the cat slashed at Campbell with hooked claws, drawing blood from his face, and then swiped again, ripping his uniform.

"That man has no sense." Father passed the spyglass back to Niall. "Does he not wonder how the rock got its name? Generations of wild cats have nested there, and that one has a litter of kittens."

Campbell swiped his arms in vain as the wild cat unleashed its fury on him, and then the Excisemen, unnerved after their experiences in the peat bog, turned and fled, with the cat in pursuit.

"Run back to Edinburgh, little gaugers," Father said. "And learn what happens when you steal Calum Gunn's whisky."

As if he had heard the words across the half-mile of bog and moorland, Campbell stopped and turned to face us. I could not see the expression on his face at that distance, but I swear I could feel the malice.

"He won't forget," I said. "He'll look for revenge."

I had no idea how prophetic my words would prove.

Catriona laughed. "He'll remember this day all his life." She looked up at Niall and smiled.

12

"Mr Gillespie!" I tapped at the side door. "Mr Gillespie, are you in?"

Pushing open the door, I stepped inside. Somebody had cleaned the corridor and removed the cobwebs to make it more presentable.

You are learning, Mr Landowner, I approved.

"Mr Gillespie! I have brought some food for you."

I stepped upstairs and cautiously opened the door to the master bedroom. The bed sat in lonely splendour, with Mr Gillespie's simple bedclothes neatly rolled up on top.

"Well," I told myself, "It seems as if Mr Gillespie's ankle has got better." I was unsure how I felt about that, for part of me had quite enjoyed caring for an invalid.

Hearing the clopping of a horse's hooves, I looked out the window in time to see Mr Gillespie riding past the house to the stables at the back.

"Mr Gillespie!" I ran down the stairs and met him as he entered the side door.

"Miss Gunn!" Mr Gillespie put down the heavy bag that he carried. "How good of you to call around again." His smile seemed genuine. "I have just been buying provisions from Aberlour."

"You could have had them sent round," I said. "The merchants would do that for a gentleman."

Mr Gillespie laughed. "Perhaps they would." He looked down at himself. "However, I do not have the appearance of a gentleman, do I?"

I shook my head. "No, Mr Gillespie," I said. Mother had always taught me to tell the truth and shame the devil. "You do not, even although you own the glen and the big house."

In truth, Mr Gillespie looked more like a gaberlunzie man than a landowner, with his battered out-of-doors clothes, his weather-tanned face, and scuffed boots.

"That was an honest answer," Mr Gillespie said.

"How is your ankle?" I wondered if I had been too honest.

"Much better, thanks to your gentle ministrations," Mr Gillespie lifted his left leg and waggled it in the air. "You see? I can move it around without difficulty." He smiled. "I would be a better host if I had more of a house than a shell."

"You cannot continue to live like this," I told him. As you see, I had inherited my father's habit of plain speaking, or perhaps that was merely my mother's honesty once again. "When winter comes along, you will need better shelter than you have here."

"Come into my kitchen," Mr Gillespie invited, lifting his bundle. "I have cleaned it up a little since you were last here." He led me into the kitchen of the house.

His phrase, "a little" was accurate. In Penrioch, everybody lived together. We performed all the household chores outside, if the weather permitted, or around the fire. In Mr Gillespie's House of the Eagle, the kitchen was separate from the living quarters. There were two huge sinks, with a broad wooden shelf around three walls and a window overlooking the back courtyard on the fourth.

"There should be a table in here," Mr Gillespie said, "and

water from the well outside. When I have a wife, I am sure she will organise some domestic staff to make things run smoothly." He gave a twisted smile. "At present—" he shrugged— "it is not looking at its best."

"It is not," I agreed.

"Do you think my intended might like it?" Mr Gillespie asked artlessly.

"I think she will demand a few changes." I wondered again who this intended might be and hoped she was a very understanding lady. Once more, I thought of Amelia Hepburn of the ready smile. "Will she be here soon?"

Mr Gillespie smiled. He put his bundle on the shelf. "She will have seen this house before evening today."

"Oh," I said. I do not know how I felt at that intelligence. "Is she visiting today?"

"She is visiting today." Mr Gillespie began to empty his bundle, taking out a bag of tea, another of coffee, some sugar and a box of ship's biscuits. "I have bought some food. It is perhaps not the best provender to offer a lady." I thought he sounded slightly ashamed, as well he might with such a poor display.

I shook my head. "It is poor fare to woo a lady," I agreed. "I presume this mysterious lady has already accepted your proposal of marriage?"

"She has not," Mr Gillespie said.

I felt a stab of something, although I was not sure what. It may have been jealousy that some strange woman would be making her home in this house that I was beginning to know so well. For one moment, I wanted to let Mr Gillespie stew in the juices of his neglect, but my Mother had said that the landowner's friendship might be valuable in future. Swallowing my pride, I forced a smile.

"When is she expected?" I asked sweetly.

"She will be here today." Mr Gillespie was maddeningly

vague. He looked around the kitchen. "I fear that my house is hardly welcoming to her."

"Indeed," I said, wishing that I had free reign on the Big House and a pot of money to call my own. I would make this house into a palace, despite the austerity of its owner. It was a dream that any woman would enjoy. Unfortunately, I was not to be that woman. Cottagers from the glen do not even dream to aspire to such heights.

"This house needs a woman's touch." Mr Gillespie seemed to have read my mind.

I nodded, not wishing to say that the house needed to be gutted, rebuilt, scoured, cleaned, decorated, and refashioned to make it liveable. "I hope that your intended has some imagination."

"Will she need imagination?" Mr Gillespie asked.

"I should say so," I said. "A woman with imagination could transform this house into something special."

"Tell me," Mr Gillespie said. "What would you do if it was your house?"

"It is not my place to say," I said, not wishing to be presumptuous. "I am only a poor farmer's daughter."

Mr Gillespie raised his eyebrows. "Even so," he said, "I have constantly been surprised by your resourcefulness in every circumstance in which you have found yourself. I use you as an example to compare others."

Unsure whether Mr Gillespie was ridiculing me, or was naturally pompous, I did not make any direct response. There was an awkward pause, during which a rising wind rattled the loose panes in the window.

"I would secure that window before I did anything," I said. "And then all the other windows and doors. They allow in the devil of a draught." I looked upwards for inspiration. "You need to repair your roof, too, and repoint the walls. Your well is old-fashioned, and in this day and age perhaps you could have water piped right into the house... "

"You've given this some thought," Mr Gillespie said.

I stopped and shook my head. "Not really," I said. "Everything I have said is obvious. You could have a beautiful house here, Mr Gillespie." I hastily added: "you and your wife."

Mr Gillespie had a slight smile on his face as he watched me. I could not read his eyes. "There will be three ladies in this house today," he said. "One of them is my intended." He indicated the jars he had bought in Aberlour. "I bought this for them."

"Oh, for goodness sake," I bristled. "You must offer your intended more than that! Where on earth did you grow up?" I could not help my quick temper, but I had never met a man who was so useless. Not only was Mr Gillespie a weakling who wished to be molly-coddled because of a sore ankle, but he was also prone to lie in his bed all day long, and now he proved himself as a disgracefully bad host.

"I grew up in the North American wilderness," he said, not in the least put out by my outburst.

"Well, that explains your accent." I had not calmed down yet, you see, or my words would have been more guarded. "What brought you to Scotland?"

"A ship," he said, and although he was smiling, I thought it best not to inquire too deeply. I knew my mother was wild with curiosity about this man, but she would have to wait until I found out more. Some things just take time.

"All right," I said. "I don't think your lady friends will like standing around in an empty house for long. They might take one look and then flee." I was about to add: "and it will serve you right," but decided it was better to keep my tongue behind my teeth.

"I think the important lady will stay longer than that," Mr Gillespie said. "She is a resourceful, and I think a stubborn, woman."

"You only *think* she will stay? Don't you know about this lady you intend to marry?"

"I don't know everything," Mr Gillespie said.

I sighed. "Men like to talk about themselves," I said, "but women like men to take some interest in them as well." I wondered if I was presuming too much.

"Carry on, please?" Mr Gillespie did not seem insulted by my advice.

"It may be a good idea to ask your lady about herself," I told him what should have been obvious to even the densest of men.

Mr Gillespie nodded. "I will do that." He looked up and frowned. "We will have to have this conversation later. I fear that I have visitors."

I heard the gentle clop of hooves on the road leading to the house. "Of course," I said. "You don't want me here when your intended calls."

No landowner would wish one of his tenants present in such circumstances. I hastily handed over the bundle I had carried from Mother's house.

"Here," I said. "It's only oatmeal porridge and bannocks and a jar of soup, but better than nothing."

"I cannot thank you enough," Mr Gillespie said. "Once again, you have saved my life."

I could see he was impatient for me to leave, so without as much as a by-your-leave, I slipped out of the side door. As I stepped outside, I saw the women had walked their horses to the stables at the back. There were only two. I thought that Mr Gillespie said he expected three women. Now, curiosity may have killed the cat, but it has enlivened my life for many years, and I was wild to see Mr Gillespie's visitors. Accordingly, I slid behind one of the many tangled bushes in his garden and waited to watch them enter.

As I waited, a hundred thoughts raced through my head. Only a couple of weeks ago, I barely thought of men. Oh, I looked at them and shared my opinions with Catriona, but that was all in fun. I never seriously considered walking out with one, let alone forming a longer-lasting relationship. Marriage was out of the question. I had no intention of tying myself down with one man or another.

More recently, though, Mother's words had made me wonder. I was twenty, coming on to twenty-one and still unmarried. Most of my contemporaries had settled down and were raising families. I remained under my father's roof, slowly growing old, with the prospect of a wizened old age, sitting by the fire all alone as the winter winds howled around the eaves.

No, I decided. I did not relish that future, and I would do something about it. Mother had her gaze fixed on Niall Grant for me, and recently I had spent some time in his company. I had thought him a rather dull dog, a man without much personality who preferred to follow rather than lead. Compared to Father, he was somewhat less than half a man, or so I believed.

However, since the ceilidh, I had seen other sides of Niall. He was a quiet man, that was certain, but he was staunch and true and had a wry sense of humour. I saw that Father used him as his right-hand man in his smuggling trips rather than any of the older men from the glen.

As well as Niall, I had met Ensign Hepburn. Although he was an officer of Militia, he was the least martial man I had ever met. I thought of him in his white underwear and could not help my smile. And that, perhaps, was Ensign Freckles' most endearing point. He made me smile, which was always a good thing in a man. I thought of my view of him trying to march with his ankles tied and a muddy smudge on his bottom, and I smiled again. Yes, Ensign Hepburn could be fun.

Thirdly, and well down the list, was Mr Gillespie. He was a landowner, and I was the daughter of a tenant farmer and whisky smuggler, so we could hardly be more different. I knew that we spoke as more-or-less equals, but I also knew that I kept a relatively firm grip on my tongue and rarely said what I was thinking. If any of my brothers had taken to his bed for a mere twisted ankle, I would have treated him to the rough edge of my tongue. I would have laced him with ridicule until he hopped back to work.

In saying that, Mr Gillespie was consistently polite to me, always treated me with respect, listened to my words and had not persecuted my father for attacking him at the ceilidh. If any of the Glen nan Gall men had been treated in such a rough manner, they would have retaliated. They might have waited for Father and cracked him over the head with a flail or a stone, or they would have cut the tails off his cattle and burned his grain.

Mr Gillespie seemed to have forgotten entirely about the incident. Evidently, the culture in North America was different to the culture in our glen.

It must have been ten minutes before I realised that the two women had gone into the house by the back door. Hearing voices from the open kitchen window and with my curiosity thoroughly aroused, I crept closer to listen. I am well aware that eavesdropping is most thoroughly immoral and those who listen seldom hear any good about themselves. However, I had seen two horsewomen pass the house, and I was honestly interested in what sort of woman would put up with the eccentric Mr Gillespie. His strange North American accent, lack of furniture and propensity for sleeping on the bare slats of a bed all added up to a highly unusual man.

I soon found out.

"I hope you intend to do something about this house, David." I had heard that voice before.

"Oh, I do, Charlotte," Mr Gillespie replied. I noted that his accent had altered. Rather than the long, pleasant drawl, he adopted when conversing with me, he now spoke in the clipped tone of the upper classes, so precise and hard-edged that each word could have cut through glass. "I fully intend to restore it to its full glory and add the most modern conveniences. I wish to repair the roof and repoint the stonework first."

"Oh, how tiresome."

Sliding my head slowly around the window, I peered inside.

Mr Gillespie was perched on the bench as though he had not a care in the world while the Charlotte woman and my friendly Amelia Hepburn stood on either side of him. I had expected Amelia, of course, as Mr Gillespie's intended, but now her presence confirmed that situation.

"I don't know how you can even talk about that sort of thing. I just give orders and leave it to the servants and tradespeople."

"Oh, do continue," my smiling Amelia said. "I am most interested to hear what you have to say. I understand the roof part, of course, but I have never heard the term "repoint" before. Pray, tell me what it means?"

As Amelia leaned forward, she placed her gloved hand on Mr Gillespie's forearm. It was a movement as delicate and subtle as a bird, yet for some reason, it invoked great indignation within me. Where had the smiling Amelia been when Mr Gillespie was lying weak and starving on his sickbed?

"I do not know," Mr Gillespie said with laughter that pealed louder than any I had yet heard from him. "It was a term I heard from one of the local women."

"Oh, la, David," Charlotte said, tapping Mr Gillespie with what I took to be a closed fan. "Do you actually talk to these people?"

"I do," Mr Gillespie said. "I admit that I find them quite amusing at times."

"I have spoken to some of them as well," Amelia Hepburn said. "I feel one must if one is to exist among them." Her laughter trilled around that room.

"I do not lower myself," Charlotte said. "I am rather of the opinion that the Donalds live in their sphere, and we live in ours, and we can only exist on either side of a glass wall. Opaque glass would suit me best." She gave a delicious shudder. "Could you imagine if we actually had one to dinner? I mean, Sir Walter Scott had that terrible Hogg fellow to his house in Edinburgh, and the ruffian actually put his feet on the sofa."

"Dear God," Amelia said. "He was a fellow Borderer, was he not?"

"He was." Charlotte agreed. "So, if a Borderer acted in such a foul manner, what would a Donald do?"

"He would likely spit his tobacco juice on the carpet," Amelia said."Or drink from the decanter at table." She giggled again. "Imagine if we had one in the house."

"Did you know that they keep their cattle inside their cottages?" Charlotte said. "They actually have them inside the cottage with them?"

"The poor cattle," Amelia said. "I always think of them as such cleanly animals."

Both women laughed as I listened at the window, feeling my anger rise at such ill-mannered, vicious, two-faced slanders against my fellow Gaels.

"What other plans do you have for your property, David?" Charlotte asked.

"I wish to bring in piped water." Mr Gillespie had been listening with a quizzical smile on his face. "After all, the well is old-fashioned, and in this day and age, we should all benefit from the most modern of conveniences."

I recognised my words and my ideas and resolved never again to speak to the vile Mr Gillespie. For all his pretended decency, he had tricked me and was using my words to impress his sweetheart.

"Piped water out here?" Charlotte sounded amazed. "Why David, that is very forward-thinking of you. Do you have any other ideas?"

"Indeed I do," Mr Gillespie said.

I shifted my stance, wondering what else I had told Mr Gillespie.

"This area is a hotbed of illicit distilling," Mr Gillespie said.

"That is why my brother is here," Amelia Hepburn said. "He fully intends to put a stop to that disgraceful practice."

"Indeed," Mr Gillespie said. "I have heard of the deeds of the South Edinburgh Militia."

I could not tell if Mr Gillespie was being sarcastic or not. I thought once more of Ensign Freckles in his white underwear and hid my now-vicious smile.

"I hope you intend driving the smugglers entirely out of the glen, David," Charlotte said.

"I have the measure of them," Mr Gillespie said. "And I have a plan that may end peat reek production in the glen forever."

I felt the rapid increase in the beating of my heart. I tried to alter my position at the window to hear better, slipped on a loose stone and fell forward, banging my head on the lowest pane.

"What was that?" Amelia said sharply. "There is somebody at the window."

"It was probably only a bird," Mr Gillespie said. "They are forever flying against the glass and knocking themselves senseless."

"No, I swear there is somebody there," Amelia said. "It will be one of the Donalds listening to our conversation."

Rapidly crawling to a patch of brambles, I lay flat on the ground, ignoring the thorns and a couple of prying wasps. I knew how difficult it was for anybody to pick out a static figure amidst vegetation, so I remained still when Mr Gillespie threw up the lower half of the window and peered outside.

"You, see?" Mr Gillespie said. "There is nobody here."

Charlotte and Amelia joined him at the window with Amelia in particular pressing close to him.

"I swear I saw somebody," Amelia said. "There was a movement that was far too large to be a bird. It was one of the Donalds. You know how they can vanish into the heather when they choose, just like Fennimore Cooper's Mohicans."

"There is no heather here," Mr Gillespie said, "and no Mohicans either."

The second the faces disappeared from the window, I crawled out of the brambles, lifted my skirt, and fled. I was not stupid enough to run without purpose, for a moving human is easily seen. Instead, I ran fifty yards and dropped into a dip of the ground where the heather stalks would hide me. From there I could see inside the House of the Eagle without the occupants observing me.

Amelia was first out and ran straight to the window. "There is nobody here," she said.

"I told you that," Mr Gillespie said. He was walking hip-to-hip with Charlotte. I watched without moving as the cold Charlotte lifted her face and kissed him on the cheek.

What? Does Amelia not mind that her friend is making love to her intended? I did not understand these Low Country people with their cold eyes and twisted morality.

As soon as they returned to the big house, I crept round to the stables and released the horses. I knew it was a senseless act of childish spite, and I did not care.

I hoped it would make me feel better. It did not. As I watched the horses run free, I only felt foolish, combined with a profound sense of hopelessness.

13

"Mr Gillespie has a plan to end peat reek in the glen, does he?" Father faced me across the breadth of the table.

"That's what he said." I nodded.

"I wonder what he has in mind." Father grinned. "The militia has not won any new battle honours so far, and the famous Malcolm Campbell was having kittens the last time I saw him."

"Campbell is a dangerous man," I said. "I am a bit afraid of him."

Father gave a short laugh. "I am sure he will be a bit afraid of me, now." He patted my shoulder. "Let me take care of Mr precious Campbell."

"Maybe so, Father," I said. "And who will take care of Mr Gillespie?"

"You will," Father said quietly. "I want you to find out what he plans to do with our glen."

"It's his glen now, Father," I said. "And I have no intention of seeing him again. His ankle is perfectly fine, so I have no excuse for visiting him."

When Father's eyes narrowed like that, I knew it was better

to do as he said. "Find out all you can," he said as if I had never uttered a word.

"Yes, father," I said.

"I'm taking a convoy down to Forfarshire this weekend," Father said. "That damned Campbell has based a whole squadron of dragoons in Perth, with a dozen riding officers and other Excisemen on patrol around the town."

"He's blocked off your customers," Mother said. "He cannot cut off the source of the supply, so he is ensuring there is no demand."

Father grinned. "There are other places and other customers." He paused for a minute as he poured out a dram of whisky for himself and one for me. "Here, Fiona. Have a sample of what we make."

I sipped at the whisky. Until that moment I had abstained, not from any sense of morality but purely because I did not fancy losing my judgement to the contents of a glass. One swallow assured me that my original decision had been correct. I felt as if I was drinking liquid flames.

"Now you know." Father had been watching me. He finished the contents of his glass in one movement. "If you have the sense I know you have, Fiona, you will drink with caution, or you will not drink at all. And you will certainly not drink when you are working with me."

"Does that mean that I am coming with you on this trip?"

"That is what it means," Father said. "You saw one of our methods on our last excursion, and you proved yourself useful. When I am too old and too infirm for this job, I want you to take over and look after me in my old age."

"You have sons," I said.

"I know that," Father said. "I also have daughters." Reaching over the table, he ruffled my hair, which both annoyed and pleased me, as he knew. His wink filled my heart.

This time, Father arranged a different diversion to entertain the militia. He had Niall drop a hint to Eilidh that there was a whisky convoy leaving for Elgin on Friday night. At nine that evening, Father sent three garrons over the Bealach Garbh with empty panniers. Twenty minutes later, he led five garrons south, watched the militia march out of Dunbeiste, and took the convoy over the Bealach nan Bo.

This time we did not stop for anything. Father had men in front and on the flanks to watch for Excisemen and pushed us along the path with no thought for sore feet or weary legs. It was only after six hard heather miles that he allowed us to stop.

"We'll rest for two hours," he said. "Lachlan, you and Niall keep watch."

"Why don't you keep watch?" Lachlan was a wiry man in his early thirties, a descendant of naked Iain Shaw who had come to the glen after the debacle of Cromdale.

"Because I need to think as well as walk," Father explained. "All you have to do is walk and watch. You don't need to use your brains." His grin was visible in the dark. "Not that you have any brains, to begin with."

Lachlan was first to laugh at Father's weak joke.

Drizzle and mist accompanied us as we set off again over deer tracks through thigh-high heather, with the surrounding heights invisible and the burns singing through the dark. Three times we upset a hiding grouse, and the "go-back" call echoed around us.

We slogged on until friendly dawn brought grey light seeping through the clouds.

By forenoon, we could see the faded blue of wild hyacinth and harebell on the lower slopes, with the golden-brown of the bracken bringing despair to the farmers.

The character of the hills changed. Soon we were among blue-grey granite with the challenging call of eagles above and a slither of scree sliding under the hooves of our horses. Father kept up the pace, listening for the call of birds that may warn of watching Excisemen and taking the convoy from cover to cover in this bleak land.

"Keep your heads below the skyline," Father warned. "And ensure the garrons are quiet." He touched the long pistol he had under his belt and watched the shifting mist in case it concealed gaugers or predatory dragoons. "They can come from an eddy of the clouds," he said. "And then things could get bloody."

"Might there be fighting?" I asked.

"If there is," Father said seriously, "I want you to get out of the way. Don't join in. Lift your skirt and run."

"But Father—"

"No buts," Father said. "No arguments this time. Out here in the wilderness, the dragoons won't take prisoners. With no witnesses, they'll think they can do as they like."

I had never heard him talk quite like that before. My jovial, devil-may-care father was stern and serious.

"Yes, Father," I said.

We ascended a rocky pass where the wind cut cruelly into our faces, stopped for a while as Niall scouted ahead to ensure neither dragoons nor gaugers were waiting in ambush, and then we mounted the head of a blustery pass. The view was stupendous. I could see a low country of fields and scattered farms, towns and villages and churches, with the sea in the far distance glittering blue and silver.

"That is Forfarshire," Father said. "And now we make our presence known." The humour was back in his expression. "And laugh in the face of the devil, the excise, Malcolm Campbell and all his men."

With the scouts reporting that there were no dragoons, Father ordered his men to produce their weapons, and in an instant, all the men and boys that I had known since childhood became Highland warriors. Some carried long-barrelled pistols, one had an actual broadsword, while most held the most formidable-looking cudgels imaginable.

I nearly laughed to see Niall flaunting his cudgel, for all the world as if he was Fingal come back to life, and wee Angus

Tulloch, who obeyed his wife's every whim, checking the lock of a pistol that looked nearly as big as he was.

I knew these men. They were farmers who would stay up all night to nurse a sick calf or spend hours cutting grain and leave a tithe to ensure the wild birds did not go hungry in winter. Now they tried to look like ferocious warriors, fit to frighten the French.

And then I realised that Bonny Prince Charlie had marched with an army very much like this, farmers and cattlemen, drovers and blacksmiths, fishermen and peddlers. Suddenly, I felt a new surge of pride in my glensmen, and wondered if all armies were the same, ordinary men thrust into gaudy uniforms and ordered to be brave for some cause that did not concern them in the slightest.

Probably, I thought and fought the waves of sadness that swept over me.

"Why the Friday face, Fiona?" Niall balanced his cudgel across his shoulder as he approached me.

"No real reason," I said. "I was just thinking about the folly of wars."

Niall smiled. "I've never been in one," he said, "and I don't intend to. Think about it, Fiona. At present, the landed class are clearing the glens of people and bringing in sheep because they make them wealthy. In a year or five or ten, these same landed gentry will be starting a war with France or Prussia or Spain or somebody else and looking for soldiers." He tapped his cudgel on the ground. "Let the sheep fight for them."

I liked Niall even more after that little speech. He was a man of sense and not some young dreamer who would disappear seeking military glory at the sight of a scarlet uniform. And then I thought of Ensign Hepburn, smiled, and patted the neck of my little garron.

"On we go then," Father said, straightened his back and marched onward, as soldierly as any officer in His Majesty's army, and with more genuine purpose as he worked to feed his family.

We arrived at the town of Brechin just as the sun slipped behind the hills. Rather than skulk in corners, Father raised his voice in a stentorian roar that could have lifted the thatch in the close-grouped houses.

"Whisky!" Father shouted. "The finest Ferintosh from the glens, made with pure Highland water and the best of barley!"

We stopped in the centre of the High Street, with the men forming a loose circle around the line of garrons, fingering their cudgels and cradling their pistols.

As always, the close buildings pressed on me. I was not happy inside a town.

"Why drink some kill-me-deadly or piss-water from the gutters?" Father was in fine form now. He yelled his wares as if he was a market salesman on some lawful venture rather than a whisky smuggler daring the Excisemen, the militia, the dragoons, the law, and the king himself. I swear I grew an inch or two in height as I swelled with pride that evening.

The first man emerged slowly with a small bottle, which Father filled for a modest fee.

"Bring your friends," Father said. "There will be no disturbance by the gaugers here, not with my boys ready for them." He indicated Niall and Lachlan, who growled menacingly and tried their best to appear tough.

I remembered Niall's shyness at the ceilidh and Lachlan cuddling his one-year-old daughter and hid my amusement.

More people appeared one at a time or in small groups, with women as likely to do the asking as men until Brechin folk eager to buy the best quality ferintosh surrounded us. After an hour, Father decided to move on.

"Good people of Brechin!" he announced. "We will be back." He led us out of that friendly little town and into the darkened countryside.

"Beat for custom," Father ordered.

One of the men used his cudgel to slowly hammer the now-empty keg at the side of his garron. We walked to the sound of a whisky-drum, awakening the farms and alerting the farmtouns and kirktouns that the glensmen were on the march.

I do not know how many places we visited that night. We walked from village to farm, from single-street hamlets of low thatched cottages to bustling communities where upwards of a hundred people lived to single crofts, known in the Low Country as pendicles, where old men and young women greeted us with joy. Nowhere were we challenged, although we saw a couple of undoubted Excisemen in the crowds that gathered to meet us. All the time, Father had the empty kegs beaten like drums and roared out that we were selling the finest Ferintosh.

Our system was the same, emptying whisky from our five and ten-gallon casks into smaller containers, from quarter anker kegs to receptacles as small as individual jugs held nervously by wrinkled old women.

"Careful you don't spill a drop," they would say and always Father was courteous to them. "It's all right, granny. If I spill any, I'll replace it free of charge."

We met a few bladdermen, small-time smugglers who carried bladders around their waists under their coats. Father filled their bladders, and they parted with silver and walked away. They would sell their bladders-full of whisky at increased prices over the next few days, spreading Father's customer base and increasing his fame.

"Cheaper for the customers to cut out the middleman," Father said. "But we don't have the time to go around every individual whisky drinker in Forfarshire. We are only testing the market this evening."

One group of hard-faced youths arrived an hour before dawn.

"Who is in charge here?" The spokesman was a thin man in his early twenties, with a city accent and a wary way about him that made me distinctly uneasy. The man at his side eyed me through a tangle of dirty blond hair, fingered a knife at his belt and smiled without humour.

"I am in charge," Father said.

"I am Peter Wallace from Dundee," the thin man said as if we should know his name. His colleagues gathered around him, eyeing our glensmen as if they were enemies. "And this is John Hay." He indicated the blond.

"Are you indeed," Father gave his most hearty smile, although I saw his hand momentarily stray to the butt of the pistol thrust through his belt.

"I'll make a deal with you," Peter Wallace said.

"And what might that be?" Father asked.

"If you supply me with thirty gallons every month, I will sell it in Dundee and split the profits with you." Wallace gave a signal, and his followers spread out, each one lingering close to one of our glensmen. Hay stood opposite me, still smiling as his gaze roved from my face to my feet before settling on my breasts.

"No deals," Father said.

"In that case, we will take all you have left," Wallace had not finished speaking before Father drew his pistol and thrust it against the Dundee man's head.

"You can take your boys and leave," Father said, "or I will let daylight into your skull."

The atmosphere altered in an instant, with our glensmen hefting their cudgels or lifting their pistols and the men from Dundee producing weapons of their own.

"Out, lads!" Wallace stepped back from the muzzle of Father's pistol, and the Dundee men followed, backing away with blustering threats and loud noises. "We won't forget you, Peatreek!"

"Keep moving," Father said and fired his pistol in the air to hurry Wallace along. The sudden crack followed by the whistle of the shot awoke half a dozen dogs, whose barking heralded the sun.

"Back into the hills," Father said, smiling.

"Who was that?" I asked.

"Peter Wallace and the Wallace gang," Father said. "They are known for ambushing smugglers and stealing their whisky. I doubt Wallace expected any resistance."

"I did not know your job was so dangerous, Father," I said.

"It can be," Father said, "but that is half the fun of the thing, jinking the gaugers, duping the soldiers, and avoiding men like Wallace."

I met his smile, but within me, I wondered if I would ever have the authority to lead a convoy of garrons over the Highland hills from Glen nan Gall to the Low Country, avoid the gaugers and soldiers and out face men such as Peter Wallace. I am only five foot two and did not have Father's confidence and presence.

Niall gave a little chuckle. "I wager that Catriona MacRae would relish this sort of life."

I looked at him, knowing that he was correct. These sorts of wild adventures would appeal to Catriona. I felt a sudden stab of jealousy, for I wished Niall to admire me, not that red-haired hussy who had delighted in baring her bottom to the gaugers.

"Of course, she would," I said. "Except that Catriona would have undressed for Peter Wallace and all his men."

Tossing my hair in the manner that Catriona had taught me, I flounced away, swinging my hips to hold Niall's attention and making sure that my skirt flicked up at the back to expose just a little too much ankle than was respectable.

Take what you like out of that, Niall Grant, and I hope it chokes you.

14

Old Man Hector Shaw died on Wednesday at the stroke of noon. We expected his death, but it was nonetheless sad and the glen united in mourning. As Hector's wife had passed away some ten years before, his children organised the funeral and the wake, with my mother helping, as she always did on such occasions.

"There will be a wake in the church hall," Mother announced to us as we gathered around the table.

"Yes, Mother, We chorused.

We had expected nothing else. There was always a wake for every death in the glen. It was a tradition as hallowed as the Sabbath and as old as time. A wake was a method of alleviating the grief and sense of loss caused by a death while lifting the spirits of the relatives of the deceased. People paid their respects, sang the deceased's favourite songs, and recounted tales of his or her exploits while in life. We all rather enjoyed a good wake, despite the associations. It was an excuse for a gathering and an opportunity to escape the drudgery of working the land.

. . .

THE WAKE WAS ON A SATURDAY, WITH OLD MAN HECTOR smartly dressed and with his beard trimmed and his hair combed so, he looked more respectable than I had ever known him.

"Now, Fiona." Mother took me to the byre of the house so only the cattle could hear her lecture. "You have to catch your man soon, and this wake is another opportunity."

"Yes, Mother," I agreed.

"Have you made up your mind for Niall Grant yet?" Mother leaned closer to me, with her eyes intent and the silver streaks in her once dark hair glittering in the light from the crusie lamps of the main house.

"Yes, Mother," I said truthfully. There was little choice, and Niall was a steady boy. Romance came second to expediency when selecting a husband, for life needed practicality more than poetry in the glen.

"Good girl!" Mother's smile always brightened my day. She pushed back a trailing hair from across her face, did the same to me and gave me a brief hug. "You will grow closer in the fullness of time."

She had a knack for reading my thoughts.

"You have some competition, I believe," Mother said. "Eilidh Mackay is still there, despite her talking to the gaugers. She is a shapely piece, and that always turns men's heads."

"Yes," I said. "And Catriona MacRae is another."

"Catriona?" Mother stepped back. "I rather like her. Well, you know what tales people spread about Catriona and her wild ways."

"Yes, Mother," I said. "Men like these wild ways as well, and Catriona was smiling to Niall when we were up the heather with Father." I did not mention Catriona's other actions, nor my own, although doubtless, Mother had already found out. Nothing much escaped the old witch.

Kindly hands had moved Old Man Hector's bed into the church hall, so he lay in state as we gathered around to wish him a fond farewell. Hector did not actually lie, for Mother thought it better if he sat up to watch the festivities in his honour and be the centrepiece rather than waiting on the sidelines.

Mother approached Dougal and Donald, the pipers. "I never see you two except at funerals, weddings, and celebrations," she said.

"Oh no." Dougal shook his head. "You never see us."

"I hope you stay around for a few days," Father said. "We could always use an extra hand or two at the final barley harvesting. There is rain threatening so the quicker the crop is in, the better."

"Oh, we can't do that," Donald was of indeterminate age, with a face hidden by a great mane of beard and eyes bright as midsummer.

"Oh no, we can't do that," Dougal echoed, swallowing about a gill of Father's whisky at a single swallow.

"And why is that, pray?" Mother asked, with her voice deceptively soft.

"It's the fingering, you see," Donald said.

"That's what it is," Dougal agreed. "The fingering."

"Tell me more." Mother sat at Dougal's side. "Tell me how the fingering prevents you from doing an honest day's work."

Donald held up his hand. "If we do manual labour," he said, "it spoils the delicacy of our touch, and then we cannot finger the chanter as well."

"That's right." Dougal lifted his fingers in turn. "Manual labour is damaging to our profession."

"I see," Mother said. "Does whisky not have the same effect?"

"Good God, no!" Donald widened his eyes at the very idea. "Whisky keeps our throats moist so we can play all the better." He swallowed another glass to prove his point. "Indeed, he said, the more whisky we drink, the better we play."

"That is why," Dougal said solemnly, "we always refuse any work that is not directly connected to whisky."

Mother glanced at Father and winked. "Gathering in the

harvest is connected to whisky," she said softly. "For our barley makes the stuff. I expect to see you the day after the Sabbath, ready to work."

"Oh, we can't do that," Donald said. "The delicacy of our touch, you see."

"I have a delicate touch too," Mother spoke ominously quietly. "And so has Calum here. So, unless you turn up, I will delicately ask Calum to speak to you..."

"And I will delicately boot you up the arse," Father said. "That won't upset the delicate touch of your fingers."

"Good." Mother smiled. "That is all settled then." She patted Dougal on the arm. "Now play for us, or I will have my man cut off your whisky supply."

With the pipers playing enthusiastically, the wake began. The drink was free, everybody in the glen crowded into the hall, and stories and songs flowed. I stood back, searching for Niall, and hoping that I could finally make the correct decision.

I had not forgotten about Ensign Hepburn. For a fleeting moment, I wondered if I should run to Dunbeiste and invite my freckled friend to the gathering so that he could meet us all. He might decide that we were a decent bunch of people and not try to interfere with the whisky distilling. I smiled at that thought and wondered if I could use the ensign to make Niall jealous. There is nothing that spurs a man so much as jealousy.

If Niall saw me in company with another man, he may well have decided that I was far better than Eilidh or that hussy Catriona. He would see that other men found me attractive, which would increase my allure in his eyes.

"Fiona!" Mother gave me a nudge that nearly knocked me down. "There is Niall, over by Hector." She pushed me in the required direction. "Go on! Talk to him!"

With my mother's gentle encouragement blistering my ears, I negotiated the hall, circling people who were dancing and wincing as Donald blew his pipes full blast beside me. I ignored Eilidh's withering glare. Niall was talking to Old Man Hector.

"Well, Hector—" Niall sipped at a small glass of whisky. "You're dead now and in the next place. You are probably watching us from your seat in heaven, laughing and wondering what all the fuss was about, eh?" He lifted his glass. "Here's to you, Hector, and good health wherever you are."

Perhaps it was Niall's toast, maybe it was the vibration of all the people dancing in the hall, or more likely there was some other explanation that I still do not understand, but as soon as Niall lifted his glass, Old Man Hector fell sideways off the bed.

"He's come alive!" somebody yelled, and all the noise in the hall stopped.

Dancers stopped dancing, drinkers halted with their glasses halfway to their lips, and courting couples did not finish their kissing and caressing. Even Donald and Dougal removed the chanters from their mouths, leaving the hiss of the bags and the dying notes of the drones to haunt the hall.

"I still owe him a shilling," Lachlan said. "Maybe he is coming to get it."

While my mother stepped forward to Old Man Hector, others shuffled toward the door. What began as a slow movement ended in pandemonium as the entire population of the glen crowded towards a door that could only accommodate one person at a time.

"Wait!" Father pushed through the crowd and stood in the doorway. "The corpse fell over! Hector is dead, and the dead cannot come back to life." He scanned the room. "Is that not correct, minister?"

I had not seen the minister in the room. Now he stood alone beside the far wall, nodding in response to Father's question.

"Yes, Mr Gunn. There is no cause for alarm."

"Pipers!" Father roared, "Wind up your pipes or whatever you do and get this blasted wake moving again!"

"Mr Gunn!" The voice did not belong to the glen. It was Malcolm Campbell, speaking from outside. "Step back inside the hall, Mr Gunn, and all you other people. Pipers, keep your pipes under control."

I looked up in dismay as Malcolm Campbell pushed into the hall, with two armed militiamen at his back, their muskets and fixed bayonets out of place amidst the mourners.

15

More militiamen thrust through the door, pushing the people of the glen before them. "Come on then, move back!"

Lachlan stepped forward. "What the hell do you think you are doing?" He tried to confront Campbell until a militia private rammed his musket butt into Lachlan's stomach.

Lachlan doubled up, gasping, and the private pushed him back.

"Enough of that," Father shouted until a corporal placed his bayonet under Father's chin and pressed.

"Get back!" Campbell seemed to be enjoying himself.

The militia formed into two lines behind him, faces immobile and bayonets pointing toward the people of the glen. I looked at them for some sign of sympathy. There was none. Their faces could have been set in flint.

"Sir, what is the meaning of this?" The minister remained in the body of his congregation. "You cannot treat the people in this manner!"

"I can, sir," Campbell said, with the mark left by the wildcat raw and livid down his face. "I am Malcolm Campbell of His

Majesty's Excise, and I have strong reasons to suspect that there is a deal of illicit whisky distilling in this glen."

"Oh." The minister looked astonished. "I have not seen any."

"No, sir," Campbell said. "I doubt that even the most hardened miscreant would plant his still in the glebe of the kirk."

"Oh, no." The minister shook his head. "I would imagine not."

"You may go, sir," Campbell said.

The minister left without a backwards glance. His congregation remained, yet hardly bereft at the sudden absence of spiritual guidance.

"The rest of you will stay put," Campbell said, "while we search every house in the clachan, investigate every patch of land and every peat stack and thatch." He touched the raw scar on his face. "By the time we have finished here, we will have found every trace of every still and every gill of illicit whisky. After that, I will personally watch as the judge locks you up for a long, long time."

I glanced at Father, who shrugged and sat down.

"Find a seat, everybody," Father said. "We can't argue with a double line of bayonets. Let Mr Campbell waste his time searching for things that don't exist, and we will continue to honour the memory of poor old Hector." Lifting a bottle, he poured himself a drink. "Or do you wish to test this whisky to see if it was taxed?"

Campbell glowered at Father. He must have known that he would face an impossible task.

The door opened again, and Captain Barrow and Ensign Hepburn stepped in.

"We have secured the village," Barrow said as Ensign Hepburn faced us. I tried to smile at my ensign. His expression did not alter.

"Then search," Campbell said. "I will come with you."

"Ensign, take over here," Barrow said. "Ensure that nobody leaves. Keep these people under control; they are smugglers at best and thieves and traitors at worst. If any of them give you trouble, do not hesitate to use force."

"Yes, sir." Ensign Hepburn touched a hand to the brim of his ridiculous shako.

Naturally, as soon as Campbell and Barrow stepped outside, I approached my ensign. "What's this all about?" I asked, smiling.

"Get back to your place!" Ensign Hepburn did not meet my smile. He pointed to the chair I had left. "Get back there and don't move!"

I felt the tension rise in that hall as the glensfolk took a collective deep breath, and the militia waited to back their young officer.

"Ensign Hepburn," I said, convinced that my freckled friend was in jest. "It's me, Fiona Gunn." I retained my smile and lowered my voice so only he could hear. "Little Pistol."

"I ordered you to get back!" Ensign Hepburn snapped, looking for all the world like a school bully and not at all like a commissioned officer in the British Army. "I have my duty to do, and I shall do it, by God."

"By God," Father said. "So you shall." Stepping forward, he put a hand on my shoulder. "Come on, Fiona."

I hesitated, still not believing that my Ensign Freckles could act in such a manner. "It's all right, Father. Ensign Hepburn is jesting."

Good God. Looking back, it is hard to believe that I could be so naïve. The young believe what they wish to believe, not what the evidence tells them.

"I don't think so, Fiona." Father hauled me back and sat me less-than-gently on my chair. "I think that Ensign Hepburn is extremely serious, and with twenty muskets at his back, it is best to sit still and do as he says. For now."

Those final two words reassured me that Father was not as defeated as he appeared. I sat down and glared at Ensign

Hepburn. I was not sure how I felt. I was apprehensive, of course, with the gaugers and the soldiers blundering around the clachan, searching for evidence of distilling. I was not unduly worried, for Father knew what he was doing, and he would have his stills or any other incriminating evidence well hidden. More important was my feeling of betrayal.

I had trusted Ensign Hepburn. I had joked with him. I had helped him when Father ambushed him at the head of the pass, and worst of all, I had liked him. I shook my head. No, that was not correct. I had more than liked him. There had been occasions when I had contemplated something deeper. Now I felt sick. My Ensign Freckles had altered from a loveable, slightly bumbling youth into a narrow-eyed professional soldier. I did not like this new ensign one bit.

For the first ten minutes, we were noisy, protesting to Ensign Hepburn and the militia. When it became evident that our complaints availed nothing against the muskets and bayonets, we became silent and glowered sullenly at the redcoats. Only the two pipers seemed unaffected as they worked steadily to remove Father's illicit whisky by pouring it down their throats.

An hour passed. Father moved his position to be beside Mother. He sat down again, folded his arms, and stared unblinkingly at Ensign Hepburn. I got a little satisfaction as the ensign coloured and looked anywhere but at Father. I remembered when the ensign and his men were running around in their underwear and wished I had not helped them.

Another hour slipped away. Father remained solid in his chair, silent as an Egyptian sphinx as he stared unrelentingly at Ensign Hepburn. In other circumstances, I would have felt sorry for the ensign. On this occasion, I experienced no such emotion. From feelings of affection, I had moved to betrayal and disappointment, to then to anger. Copying Father's stance, I added my glare to his and noticed that Mother was doing the same.

"Show these sojers what we think of them," Mother snapped,

and one by one, the folk of the glen sat squarely on their stools or benches and looked directly at Ensign Hepburn.

I felt some savage satisfaction as he shifted and looked away, unable to face the concentrated disapproval of Glen nan Gall. The private soldiers and even some of the bitter-eyed sergeants began to look nervous. The silent contemptuous stare of the Gael is a potent weapon.

By the time Captain Barrow and Malcolm Campbell returned, the militia was unsettled, and Ensign Hepburn was scarlet with embarrassment. The people of Glen nan Gall were in control of the church hall, despite the muskets and bayonets of the militia.

Campbell carried something inside a canvas bag.

"Let them go," Barrow said shortly.

"What did you find, Captain?" Father asked.

"Nothing," Barrow said. "Let them go."

"Not all of them," Campbell contradicted. "Keep the Gunn family here."

I stared at Father, who gave me a wink and remained seated as all the others stood.

"Calum," Mother said, "what is this?"

"Sit still," Father said. "It is some ploy of Campbell's to unsettle us. The more we react, the more pleasure he will have."

"Do you wish the children as well, Mr Campbell?" Mother asked.

"No," Campbell said. "You may send them away. Except her." He nodded to me. "Your oldest daughter must remain."

"I'll care for them," Catriona said. "They'll be safe with me."

"We're with you, Calum." Lachlan said as he and Niall, bless them, stood at our side. "What do you wish us to do?"

"I wish you to return to your homes and live your lives," Father told him. "Let events take their course."

Niall stamped his feet on the ground. "We have weapons," he said. "We can get the redcoats out of the glen."

"We have, and we could," Father agreed. "And in three days,

there will be an entire regiment from Fort George or Aberdeen, regular infantry, cavalry, and cannon. The South Country men do not care for the Gaels. They will call it rebellion and waste the glen, killing who they do not imprison, and they will justify it all in the name of the king. Remember the republican rising of 1820." He smiled. "Thank you, Lachlan and Niall, but I do not want the blood of the glen on my head. Go, now."

There were other offers of help and support, to which Father gave the same reply. Gradually the people of Glen nan Gall left the hall, so we sat there alone, with Campbell and the militia watching us.

"Are you sure you are safe behind your escort, Campbell?" Mother asked. "Twenty bayonets to hold one man, one woman and a girl? You must be very afraid of three unarmed Highlanders."

"We have searched the clachan and all the surrounds," Campbell sounded triumphant. "And we found no trace of a black bothy."

Father said nothing.

"You hide them well, Gunn."

Father still said nothing. I copied his example, feeling very uncomfortable. Despite the chill of the evening, perspiration trickled down my back. Old Hector lay on his bed, a dead silent witness as all the militia looked ahead.

Ensign Hepburn savagely reprimanded a private who dared to cough.

"Now that we are alone—" Campbell conveniently discounted the militia— "we can talk freely. Pulling up a bench, he sat down directly opposite us, with his long legs crossed and the butt of his pistol visible at his hip. He placed that canvas bundle in his lap and patted it as if it was a household cat. "I had your lands searched and found nothing."

Father nodded.

"And then I ordered your houses searched as well."

I felt Mother stiffen. "I hope you left the place tidy," Mother said. "If there is anything broken or missing, I will expect payment from your own purse, Mr Malcolm Campbell."

"Nothing is broken or missing," Campbell said smoothly. "As well as defrauding the government through illegal distilling, I had intelligence that there was a thief among the Gunns."

"There is no thievery in my family," Mother said.

She was quite correct. Although we would all happily distil whisky without paying tax or poach a fish or a deer from land that legally belonged to another, we did not count such actions as theft. Highlanders had distilled whisky for centuries before greedy governments decided to tax it to fund foreign wars, while the Bible stated that God had placed fish and deer on the land for us to eat. Landlords were stealing from us, not us from them.

"That was not what I heard," Campbell said. "And that is not what a search of your home found." Opening the canvas bag on his knee, he pulled out the silver teapot that Mr Gillespie had given me.

"That's mine!" I said at once.

No sooner had I stood to claim my possession than the militia sergeant had his bayonet at my throat.

"Sit down!" He roared as if I was a hundred paces away rather than at the sharp end of his weapon. "Don't threaten the Excise officer."

Father eased me back to my seat. "If you threaten my daughter again," he said quietly to the sergeant, "you will never see another dawn."

"Sit down, both of you," Mother said. "We will sort this out without threats or violence. And you," she addressed the sergeant, "should be ashamed of yourself, threatening a young girl with a musket and bayonet. And you call yourself a soldier! Go and fight the French or somebody rather than harassing innocent people attending a wake. Shame on you! Shame on you all, disrespecting the dead!"

Campbell had listened, with a small smile on the edges of his lips. "Thank you, sergeant. You may return to your position."

Feeling sicker than I had for many years, I sat on my chair. Campbell continued, with the scar on his face now vivid. I wished that the wildcat had slashed his throat open rather than merely tearing his cheek. Next time, I vowed, next time, I would have no sympathy for these people, be they Excisemen, militia or the king himself.

"Do not tell me that this is a family heirloom, and do not tell me that you bought this from a travelling tinker."

Mother placed a restraining hand on my arm. "It is not a family heirloom, and we did not buy it from a travelling tinker," she confirmed.

"Then tell me, pray, from where it came?" He directed his question at me. "You claimed ownership of this teapot, Fiona, so you had best explain its provenance."

"Explain its what?" I had never heard the term before.

"Tell me where you got it from," Campbell said.

"Mr Gillespie gave it to me," I said. I held out my hand to have my teapot returned.

"Mr Gillespie gave it to you," Campbell said. "And why would Mr Gillespie give you, a smuggler's daughter, something of such value?"

"He is my friend," I said.

Campbell's laugh echoed around the hall. "I hardly think that the owner of this glen would befriend the daughter of its most notorious smugglers." He shook his head. "No, Miss Gunn. You stole this." He raised his voice. "Fiona Gunn, I arrest you in the Kings name and charge you with theft. Take her away."

When Father and Mother rose in protest, the militia surged forward and surrounded them. Within a minute, the redcoats hustled me out of the hall, a prisoner.

16

Wherever I looked, there were soldiers. They surrounded Penrioch and stood in small groups outside every cottage. Their uniforms were red as blood, their bayonets glittered in the moonlight, and they were as faceless as the granite of the high peaks.

What few glensfolk were there could only stare as one of Campbell's gaugers produced a pair of heavy handcuffs and fastened my wrists together. Then I was pushed along the road with armed militiamen all around and my heart sinking to its lowest ever level.

"I did not steal anything," I said. "Ensign Hepburn, you know me. You know I would never steal anything."

Ensign Hepburn turned his head slightly. "The prisoner will remain silent," he said.

"Do I have to wear these?" I held up my wrists, where the heavy manacles were chafing the flesh.

"If the prisoner utters another word, she will be gagged," Ensign Hepburn said.

"Best keep quiet, miss," one of the older privates advised. "You don't want a gag stuck in your mouth."

"I am innocent!" I wailed, quite put out by this ill-treatment.

"Gag the prisoner," Ensign Hepburn ordered, with his freckles merging into an orange-brown streak that stretched from cheek to cheek across his nose.

I no longer found his freckles appealing.

"What?"

Two privates grabbed hold of me, and a third placed a leather belt around my mouth, fastening it behind my head.

"That will keep you quiet," one said, pulling the belt tight so the leather cut into my mouth. "Yap-yap-yapping there as if anybody cared what a bloody thieving Donald had to say."

With the taste of leather in my mouth and tears in my eyes, I stumbled along the path to Dunbeiste. I looked around, seeing only unfriendly faces, and hearing the regular crunch-crunch of boots on the ground.

"Get a move on!" a harsh voice snarled, and somebody shoved me in the back.

I wished I was back home with my brothers and sisters. I wished the militia and the gaugers had never come to Glen nan Gall. I wished that somebody would come and chase these South Country intruders away so that life could get back to normal.

None of these events occurred. I was a prisoner of these English-speaking, cold-eyed strangers, and there was nothing I could do to save myself.

The sentries presented arms as we marched past the gate of Dunbeiste, and within five minutes, my escort dragged me to a flight of stairs and deposited me in a small cell.

"This used to be the castle dungeon," the sergeant told me. We use it as the guard room now. You'll be safe here until the captain decides what to do with you. Here." He stepped forward and removed my shackles. "There's no need for these things."

I stared at him, unable to speak because of my gag and unable to retaliate against a hundred uniformed men. When the heavy door banged shut, I sat on the stone-flagged floor and wept, as miserable as I had ever been in my life and very much more alone.

That was the joy of living in the old Highland glens. We were never alone unless we chose to be. We were a clan, a family, and worked together as a community with everybody looking out for each other and nobody left out. There was never any time to be melancholy or reason to be lonely.

Now, trapped in that dark place of stone walls and a stone floor, I was truly alone for the first time in my life, and I did not like the experience one little bit. The only consolation was that I could remove the belt from my mouth. I can still taste that leather many years later. Even the smell of leather is something I cannot abide.

I WAS USED TO THE LONG DARK HIGHLAND WINTERS, SO THE absence of light was not fearful, while the scurrying of mice was no hardship. It was the lack of company that pressed upon me that night. Loneliness combined with the stuffiness of the air and the numbing confusion of why I was there in the first place, forced me into utter dejection.

I may have slept. I may not. I only remember the door being thrown open and the yellow glow of a lantern, with the shadowy shape of a burly soldier holding it high.

"Breakfast," he said without ceremony and threw in a metal tray of thin gruel. "Eat it quickly because an officer is coming to see you in a minute."

"An officer?" I said, wild for any kind of companionship, and then the door slammed shut again, and I heard the scrape of a key in the lock.

I ate the disgusting mess that the soldiers called breakfast, and then the door opened again, and Ensign Hepburn stood there with a private soldier on either side of him.

"Ensign Hepburn," I said.

"Well now, Miss Gunn." The ensign did not enter my place of

confinement. "This is a pretty pickle you have got yourself into, is it not?" He was smiling again, with his freckles merging.

"I stole nothing," I said, "and I ask you to release me." I had resolved not to bluster or fume but to act in a rational, civilised manner. Any retaliation could wait until later. I am a Gael, and we nurse our vengeance with patience that can span generations.

"You know that my duty forbids me to do that, Miss Gunn."

"Your duty!" I snapped and then took a deep breath of the damp, foul air. "Ensign Hepburn," I said and forced a smile that was utterly false. "Is there any need for two armed guards when you speak to me? We have known each other for weeks now, and you must be aware that I am not going to leap at you like Walter Scott's Rob Roy or like some Fingalian hero." Although he may have read Rob Roy, I doubted if this southern officer had ever heard of Fingal, despite MacPherson's attempts to introduce the Highland hero to the world. "Anyway, I am rather diminutive to overpower a strapping man such as you, as well as only a female."

Good God, the lies I have told in my life! I would lay odds on my ability to deal with this South Country buffoon in any situation. However, I was not so confident that I could escape Dunbeiste with its garrison of redcoats. Anyway, I still trusted that I could persuade Ensign Freckles that the whole thing was a mistake and secure my release by civilised means. Ensign Hepburn nodded. "You two men may dismiss," he said.

"Very good, sir." The privates turned around and marched away.

"Now, Miss Gunn, I must warn you that your position is grave in the extreme."

"Miss Gunn?" I raised my eyebrows as enticingly as I could, considering I was standing within a foul dungeon in clothes that were crushed and already encrusted with dirt. "Whatever happened to Little Pistol?"

Ensign Hepburn did not respond directly. "I have my duty to do, Miss Gunn."

"Now, Andrew," I used his Christian name in an attempt to

unsettle him a little. "You know that I am no thief. Mr Gillespie gave me that teapot as a gift."

"A justice of the peace will be arriving later today." Ensign Hepburn ignored everything that I said. "And the procurator fiscal as well. If he decides there is sufficient evidence for a trial, you will remain locked up until the circuit court in Perth."

"What?" The talk of procurator fiscals and circuit courts shocked me. "You know I am innocent, Ensign."

"It was my duty to inform you what was happening," Ensign Hepburn said. "And I have done my duty. Now, I advise you to prepare yourself, Miss Gunn, for things do not look favourable for you."

"What does that mean?" I wailed.

Without answering, Ensign Hepburn gave a curt, formal bow and withdrew.

I sat down on the thin straw mattress that was the only comfort in my dungeon. It was not one of these horrible bottle-shaped dungeons that some old castles have, but a rectangular room with a stone-flagged floor and stone walls. The door was of solid oak, studded with iron, and the only light seeped through a tiny square window high above my head.

I put my head in my hands and wondered what was to become of me.

I could not judge the passage of time in that fearful place. Sometimes I sat on the mattress, and then I would stand and walk the five paces from the door to the back wall and the five paces back. My head was in confusion, worrying, wondering, and dreading my next visitor.

It may have been the early afternoon of the next day when the door opened again. Two serious-faced men walked in. One was a distinguished-looking gentleman with impressive white whiskers who I guessed was the Procurator Fiscal. The other was Mr Snodgrass, the Factor of the estate.

"You are Fiona Gunn." The Procurator Fiscal did not waste time. "And you are accused of theft."

I nodded. "I am Fiona Gunn," I said. "I am innocent of theft."

"I have reviewed your case," the Procurator Fiscal said, "and I believe that it is sufficient evidence to charge you."

"I am innocent," I said.

"That is for the jury to decide." Mr Snodgrass chipped in. "In the absence of Mr Gillespie, I will act his agent and prosecute you." He glanced around my dungeon. "It is my unpleasant duty to advise you to get used to your accommodation. I foresee a future for you in similar chambers."

I cannot describe my state of mind when that terrible door closed. I slumped down on my mattress, placed my head in my hands, and wept. I had never been prone to despair or feeling sorry for myself but, I was as depressed as ever in my life. I had not liked Snodgrass when I met him in Aberlour. I liked him much less when I knew he was to be my prosecutor.

I cannot remember anything notable about the next few days. I could not even tell you how long I was in the dungeon, for every day followed the same routine, and days merged into a monotonous greyness. I do remember the day the door opened, and two well-dressed men stood there. I recognised them as the Sheriff Officers who had accompanied Campbell on his abortive attempt to find Father's stills. I hoped they did not remember my actions on that day.

"Come on, Miss Gunn," the younger one said. "I am Charles Horne, and this is James Mitchell. We are Sheriff Officers, and you are coming with us."

That was all the warning I got. There was no time to prepare, no time even to properly wash. One minute I was sitting in the damp gloom of my dungeon, and the next, these two burly men were hustling me through Dunbeiste.

"Put your hands out," the older of the men said.

Dazed after so long alone, I obeyed without question. The handcuffs again nipped my wrists, somebody pushed me hard in the back, and I blinked in sudden daylight.

A group of private soldiers watched as I staggered out with my now-filthy clothes inadequate against the autumnal rain and my hair a tangled mess on my head. I looked in vain for a friendly face or even for Ensign Hepburn. I failed on both counts, and within a few moments, the Sheriff Officers were pushing me into a closed coach and ordering the driver to whip up his horses.

Although that was the first time I had ever been inside a coach, the novelty was entirely lost on me, given the circumstances. We moved off with a sudden jerk, and I just had time to peer outside before one of the sheriff officers pulled down the blind and blocked all view of the glen. I had time to see my family standing outside Dunbeiste, with Father staring at the coach and Mother with her arms wrapped around my siblings. Four red-coated soldiers kept them back with bayoneted muskets.

"Mother!" I shouted.

"Keep your mouth shut!" Horne, the younger of the Sheriff Officers, snarled.

I remember very little about that journey. Handcuffed and stuck beside two grim-faced men, I remained silent, lost in my thoughts, and they were dark and dismal. I knew I was innocent of any theft, yet I had no confidence in the legal process for any Gael. It was only seventy years since the last of the Jacobite Risings, and we were at the height of the Highland Clearances, where sheep and deer were deemed more important than men and women. We were not wanted in our own land and knew it.

As the crow flies, it is no great distance between Glen nan Gall and Perth, where the circuit judge presided over his autumn court. By coach, it was considerably longer as the road had to circle the hills before descending to the Low Country and into the town itself. Three times on that dismal journey, I tried to talk to my jailers, and on each occasion, they answered me with brutal insults. I did not pursue a fourth attempt.

"Out," Horne said and pulled me from the coach. I barely

had time to see the massive jail before the Sheriff Officers rushed me inside.

"Another for you," they reported to a scowling, bald-headed man who I presumed to be the jailer.

"That's twenty for tomorrow then," the jailer said. His grin revealed brown stumps of teeth. "Is she ripe for hanging?"

"Theft from a landowner," Mitchell said. "Sign for her." He handed over a bundle of documents, and the jailer scanned them briefly, leaned them on a slanting desk and then scrawled with a goose-wing quill.

"Ten years transportation then," the jailer said. "That will be Van Diemen's Land for you, my girl." My case seemed to amuse him. Overcome with the horror of my situation, I said nothing.

A female turnkey arrived, put a hard hand on my shoulder and hustled me up a flight of worn steps to a tiny cell.

"You need a wash," she said. "You're stinking."

I agreed, and within twenty minutes, the turnkey brought me a wooden basin and a tub of clear water with a cloth. "Hurry up," she said and handed over a small bar of soap. That was the first small act of kindness anybody had shown me for days, and I could not help my tears.

"It's no good crying," the turnkey said. She was a middle-aged woman with grey hairs and eyes that had seen a deal of human suffering. "The judge does not know the meaning of sympathy. What did you do?"

"Nothing," I said as I stripped to wash.

"Nobody ever has," the turnkey said. "What are you accused of doing?"

"Theft," I said.

The turnkey nodded. "Did you plead innocence?"

"Yes," I said, enjoying the clean water despite my situation.

"It will be a jury trial then," the turnkey said. "Judges don't like jury trials. They prefer a guilty plea, for that saves them time and trouble. If you plead guilty, they give a lesser sentence."

"I am innocent," I said.

"That matters not a whit," the turnkey said. "Judges want a quick finish, so they get along to their dinner. Best change your plea to guilty, and you'll be free in a few years."

"I am innocent," I repeated.

"As you wish," the turnkey said. "Come along now. I don't have all day."

Rather than a cell to myself, the turnkey placed me in a chamber with three other women, who looked up without interest as I joined them.

Two were prostitutes from the lowest class of society, and the third had murdered her baby. She spent the entire time alternating between crying at what she had done and praying that the judge would spare her the rope. The two prostitutes spoke amongst themselves in the filthiest conceivable language, laughed at the unhappy murderess, and openly discussed me.

"I am accused of theft," I said.

"What value?" One asked. She was a devil-eyed, black-haired creature with claws like a wildcat and a dress so low-cut that it was indecent.

"I don't know," I replied.

"Was it above or below five shillings?" Her questions came out like bullets as her companion, a greasy-haired strumpet with few teeth, sang a song so bawdy it would make marine cringe.

"I don't know," I repeated. "It was a silver teapot."

"Above five shillings," the black-haired one said at once. "Plead guilty and say you needed the money to pay doctor's bills for a sick child. That may save you from the gallows."

"I am innocent," I said.

"I believe you," the prostitute said. "You don't look like a thief."

I lay on my side on a thin straw mattress that harboured things that kept me awake with their rustlings, and I greeted the morning with a host of raw red bites and a horrible feeling of foreboding.

"What happens now?" I asked my bawdy companions.

"It's judge Lord Cochrane," the greasy-haired woman said. "I had his son once, outside the Town House in Dundee. A dirty little beggar he was too."

"Everybody had his son," the black-haired prostitute said. "He got a dose, and now Cochrane hates all women."

That sounded ominous. I felt any slender hope vanish as the turnkey gave me a plate of soup and a hunk of hard bread for breakfast and said I would appear in mid-morning.

"Lord Cochrane," she sounded offhand. "He's not quite a hanging judge, but he's no sympathy for women."

I could not eat my breakfast and fought my tears.

Two tall men escorted me from my cell into a large room, busy with culprits and lawyers. It was here that, for the first and only time, I met the solicitor who was responsible for my defence.

"Fiona Gunn?" He was a fussy little man with a high, old fashioned collar and pince-nez glasses. "Thank God. I could not find you in the crowd. "I am Mr Todd, your defence. What did you steal?"

"Nothing," I said. "I am innocent."

"Of course you are," Mr Todd said. "Now we have to convince the judge. Tell me your story."

I related all that had happened as he listened and scribbled notes on a pad of paper with a short quill. "I see," he said. "The landowner, this Mr Gillespie, found the silver teapot in an empty room and handed it to you."

"Yes, exactly that," I said, pleased that somebody seemed to believe me.

"Well, that is hardly plausible, is it?" Mr Todd said. He shrugged. "If that's the best you can do, it looks bad for you." He shrugged. "We'll try it and see what Lord Cochrane thinks." He lowered his voice. "Our Lordship is a bit liverish today, so I wish you good luck."

That was all the time I had to consult my defence before he

scurried away and a burly man snarled at me to sit and behave myself, or it would be the worse for me.

"Fiona Gunn!" I heard my name called, and somebody tall and imposing took hold of my arm and propelled me through a massive door into the courtroom.

I wanted to die.

17

I do not know what I had expected. I had heard of courtrooms and judges, but that was the first time I had ever seen one. The room was smaller than I had thought it would be, and the place I stood was closer to the judge and the jury than was comfortable.

I was in a sort of wooden box, with little spikes around me, presumably to prevent me from leaping up and attacking the judge. In truth, I was shaking so much I could scarcely stand, let alone leap, and the number of hard-faced men around would have intimidated Donald Dhu, let alone a young girl from the glens.

I cannot remember the start of my trial. I only remember answering "yes" or "no" to the questions the judge or the prosecution threw at me. Lord Cochrane was nothing like I had thought. Rather than a huge man with glaring red eyes and a wig, he was an elderly, benign-looking fellow with a sad face. The wig was there, though, looking larger than its wearer, and he wore a ridiculous red cloak trimmed with fur, if I remember correctly.

"You say that Mr Gillespie handed you this silver teapot as a gift," Snodgrass, the prosecutor, said.

I took a renewed dislike to this sneering-faced man with his acid tongue and a swagger when he abused his position of power to badger people who had no means of retaliation.

"Yes," I said. I realised that it would be better if I treated Snodgrass with respect and call him "sir", but my Highland pride forbade me to bow before a man whose sole function in life seemed to be to condemn me.

"Why would he do that?" the prosecutor asked.

"Maybe because I had brought him food and bound up his damaged ankle," I said.

"Is this mysterious Mr Gillespie available to verify your alleged good deeds?" Snodgrass looked around the courtroom, perhaps hoping to see Mr Gillespie materialise from the air or pop out from under one of the jury's coats.

"I don't know," I said, truthfully and crossly. "I have no idea where Mr Gillespie might be. I have been locked up on a charge for something I did not do." I felt my temper rising. I thought perhaps the spikes around me served a useful purpose after all, as I contemplated reaching out, grabbing the prosecutor, and banging his face...

Lord Cochrane started speaking. "The panel will kindly moderate her language when replying to questions."

The panel? That must be me.

"Yes," I said.

"I believe Mr Gillespie is in London on business," Lord Cochrane informed the prosecutor.

"How convenient that the panel's only possible witness is elsewhere," sneering Snodgrass said.

Mr Todd stood up. "We cannot blame Miss Gunn for the actions of Mr Gillespie."

Thank you, Mr Todd.

I could have hugged him for trying. Standing accused in a Lowland court was a very lonely place for a young Highland girl. I quickly scanned the audience, hoping for a friendly face. I saw nobody that I knew.

Have Father and Mother abandoned me? I knew they would not do that. *But, where are they?*

"I do not blame Miss Gunn for the absence of Mr Gillespie," Snodgrass said. "I only blame her for attempting to use a witness who cannot be found."

The audience laughed at this nasty little joke, and the prosecutor continued. "In the absence of Mr Gillespie's testimony that he did not give Miss Gunn his prized teapot, for whatever mysterious reason, I will attempt to ascertain the panel's character by other means."

I waited, wondering what these "other means" might be and how on earth this slimy evil, hectoring man could find out anything about my character.

"Call Miss Charlotte Barrow."

Miss Charlotte Barrow? That must be Captain Barrow's sister.

I watched as she took the oath on a Bible and stood in the witness box. As always, she stood proud, with her back straight and her clothes immaculate.

"You are Miss Charlotte Barrow?" Snodgrass asked.

"I am, sir," Charlotte Barrow replied in a clear, calm voice.

"Do you know the accused?"

Charlotte Barrow favoured me with a look that should have consigned me to the deepest pits of Hell. "I know of her, sir," she said. "I believe I have seen her in Glen nan Gall."

"Thank you, Miss Barrow. Would you be kind enough to tell the court of the circumstances when you saw her in Glen nan Gall?"

"There were two occasions that I recall," Charlotte Barrow said. "The first was when I first arrived. My companion, Miss Hepburn and I were riding to Dunbeiste Castle, where my brother commands the garrison, and this woman accosted us."

"Did you speak to her?" Snodgrass asked.

"I did not, sir. I am not in the habit of spending time with stray women. She was sitting on a wall, dressed in utter rags, with her feet and lower legs quite bare." Charlotte Barrow graced the prosecutor with a faint smile. "She is hardly the sort of person with whom one would wish to spend time. Would you?"

Snodgrass looked me up and down as if I was a piece of rotting meat. "Not by choice," he said. "And I doubt that any member of the jury would either."

I wondered if I should remind him of his proposal to me when I tried to pay the rent. I knew that nobody would believe the word of a Highland girl when opposed to somebody her supposed social superior.

"I object," Mr Todd intervened at last.

Lord Cochrane nodded. "Yes indeed, Mr Todd. Pray continue, Mr Snodgrass."

Snodgrass. I knew I would always remember that name. I vowed to get back at Mr Snodgrass, somehow, some time in this life or the next.

"Thank you, my Lord." Snodgrass gave a smarmy smile. God, I hated that man. "Now, Miss Barrow, you have related your first encounter with the panel. Could you tell the members of the jury about your second?"

I waited, wondering when this second encounter might have been as I had no recollection of speaking to this woman.

"It was a few weeks later." Charlotte Barrow screwed up her face as if trying hard to remember. "We were within Mr Gillespie's residence in Glen nan Gall…"

"We?" Mr Snodgrass pounced on the word. "Could you tell the members of the jury who else was there?"

"Yes, of course." Charlotte Barrow faced the fifteen members of the jury. "I was present with Miss Amelia Hepburn and Mr Gillespie."

Mr Snodgrass nodded, allowing the jury time to digest the information. "Are we to presume that you know Mr Gillespie well, then?"

"Oh, indeed." Charlotte Barrow said. "I understand that Mr Gillespie and I are to be married."

The jury gave a collective sigh. One or two smiled at Charlotte as if pleased to hear that such an eminently respectable young woman had ensured her future. I knew then that they would believe whatever she said, while the words of a Highland tyke with a broad Gaelic accent such as myself would be treated with the greatest of suspicion.

I had thought it was Amelia who was to marry Mr Gillespie, and all the time, it was this stuck-up witch. No wonder they had kissed.

I hoped she caught the plague.

With that realisation came a second sensation, one of sinking despair. Somewhere inside me, I had hoped that Mr Gillespie would ride to my rescue, like Ivanhoe or Lancelot. With Mr Gillespie betrothed to Miss Barrow, that would not happen. He would support his sweetheart.

I was alone.

Mr Snodgrass again waited for the jury to absorb this new intelligence. "Congratulations, Miss Barrow. I am sure it will be a happy match. Would you tell us, please, if you believe you know Mr Gillespie well?"

"I believe I know him very well indeed," Charlotte spoke with confidence.

"Would you say, given your close knowledge of Mr Gillespie's habits and tastes, that he would be likely to befriend the panel?"

Charlotte spared me one contemptuous glance. "I would think that highly unlikely."

"Thank you, Miss Barrow." Snodgrass threw me a disgusted look. "Now tell the jury where you saw the panel."

"Mr Gillespie, Miss Hepburn, and I were talking in the kitchen when we heard a noise outside the house," Charlotte said. "We ran to the window, and I got the distinct impression that somebody was hiding in the bushes."

I tightened my mouth, remembering that incident exactly.

"Did you see anybody, Miss Barrow?" Snodgrass asked.

"I am not entirely sure," Charlotte said.

"I am confident the jury appreciates your desire not to

incriminate anybody unjustly." Snodgrass gave more credit to Charlotte than she deserved. "However, I must press this matter. Did you think you saw somebody skulking in the bushes outside the house?"

"I thought I did," Charlotte said.

"Did you think it could have been a woman?" Snodgrass asked.

"Yes," Charlotte said with a firm nod of her perfectly poised head. "I would say so. There was not sufficient room in the bushes for a man to hide, but a woman could."

"Particularly a small made woman," Snodgrass indicated my lack of height.

"I would say so," Charlotte said.

"Thank you, Miss Barrow. I have no more questions."

I hoped that Mr Todd would tear Charlotte's imaginings to shreds, but instead, he merely asked her to confirm that she was uncertain about what she had seen.

"Now, Miss Barrow," Snodgrass said. "I wish you to identify this piece of evidence." He produced my silver teapot, held it up for the jury to see and then passed it to Charlotte.

"I cannot identify it," Charlotte said. "I have never seen it before."

"Thank you for your honesty," Snodgrass said smoothly. "I would ask you to examine it thoroughly."

Charlotte did so, turning it over in her gloved hands.

"Can you see any distinguishing features?" Snodgrass asked.

"There are two," Charlotte said. "There is an Edinburgh hallmark on the underside and a coat-of-arms on the front."

"Yes, Miss Barrow. And can you identify the coat-of-arms?"

"I can," Charlotte said. "It is the same design as is carved above the front door of the big house in Glen nan Gall."

Mr Todd pointed out that I had never denied that the silver teapot came from the big house. Some of the jurymen scribbled a few notes. None gave me any encouragement.

Amelia Hepburn was next up, and Snodgrass asked her when

she had first met me. She confirmed what Charlotte had said, threw me a condescending smile and added that "Miss Gunn was a most personable girl, considering her humble background."

Snodgrass pounced on that hint with claws as predatory as any hunting eagle. "Considering her humble background, Miss Hepburn? Could you explain to the gentlemen of the jury what you mean?"

"Oh, I did not intend any slur on Miss Gunn," Amelia said. "I am sure she has no connection to the behaviour of her father."

"Miss Hepburn, I must press you for further information."

"Oh." Amelia contrived a most useful blush. "Miss Gunn's father is Calum Gunn, and my brother, Ensign Hepburn, is convinced that he is the leading whisky smuggler of Glen nan Gall."

The jury shifted in their seats, looking at me with even greater suspicion than they had when first I arrived.

"There is no proof of that," Mr Todd tried to salvage my case. "And Miss Gunn is not on trial for the supposed crimes of her father."

"Indeed not, Mr Todd," Lord Cochrane said. "The gentlemen of the jury will disregard that piece of evidence."

They may, I thought, but it was more likely that they would not. I expected that the gentlemen of the jury would regard me as a member of an outlaw family and all the more liable to steal. I looked away, wondering for how long Lord Cochrane would jail me.

Snodgrass paused for a few moments before calling his final witness. I started when he asked for Eilidh Mackay. While Charlotte and Amelia had no particular reason to dislike me, Eilidh was no friend of mine. She came to the stand dressed in her Sunday best with shoes upon her feet and her hair gleaming. She looked the very model of respectability compared to my ragged gaberlunzie appearance.

"You are Eilidh Mackay?" Mr Snodgrass asked quietly.

"Yes, sir," Eilidh said demurely, smiling shyly upwards from her gleaming gold hair.

"And you live in the same clachan of Penrioch in Glen nan Gall as the panel, as the accused?" Snodgrass retained his gentle voice.

"Yes, sir," Eilidh said.

"I believe that your mother brings up both you and your brother," Snodgrass said, "while your father died serving his country."

"Father was a soldier," Eilidh said.

"You should be proud of him," Snodgrass raised his voice. "In my other capacity of the Factor of Glen nan Gall, Eilidh's mother has never been remiss in paying her rent, and the family has never been suspected of indulging in whisky distilling or any other illegal activity. In fact, they are model tenants."

"Thank you, Mr Snodgrass." Lord Cochrane nodded.

"Now, Miss Mackay, I have you here as a character witness. Do you understand what that means?"

"Not really, sir," Eilidh said.

"It means I am going to ask you questions to see what sort of person the accused, Miss Gunn is."

Eilidh scowled at me. "Yes, sir."

"How long have you known Miss Gunn?" Snodgrass asked.

"All my life, sir," Eilidh said.

"And in that time, to the best of your knowledge, has Miss Gunn ever done anything dishonest?"

"Oh, yes, sir." Eilidh gave me a look of triumph as she realised what power she suddenly had. "She stole my sweetheart, Niall Grant, sir."

As Snodgrass looked momentarily dumbfounded, Lord Cochrane and half the jury broke into spontaneous laughter. I did not find it amusing in the slightest.

"I see," Snodgrass said. "Do you know of any other acts of Miss Gunn of which society might disapprove?" As Eilidh looked confused, Snodgrass explained further. "Has Miss Gunn done anything dishonest? Has she broken the law?"

Eilidh wrinkled her nose, trying to think of anything to incriminate me. At last, she shook her blonde head. "Not really, sir."

"She did not join her father in his illicit whisky distilling, for instance," Snodgrass said desperately.

"Oh, yes, sir, she did that all right." Eilidh gave a smile, pleased that she could help the kind Mr Snodgrass. "She went on a couple of trips with him, selling whisky in Perth and Brechin. Why I believe that she helped sell whisky to some of the gentlemen in Perth."

"We need say no more about that," Snodgrass said hurriedly, in case some of the jurymen were recipients of Father's peat reek. "The important point here is that Miss Gunn knowingly broke the law on at least two occasions. Can we believe her when she says she did not steal this teapot?"

"It is possible that my client was coerced into helping her Father," Mr Todd tried his best to mitigate my guilt.

"Miss Gunn," Lord Cochrane said. "You are not on trial for distilling or distributing illicit whisky. I must, however, remind you that you are under oath."

"Yes, Your lordship." Somewhat belatedly, I attempted to appear meek.

"Did your father force you into helping him? Did he threaten you in any way, either by force or because of family loyalty?"

Knowing that every eye in that courtroom was fixed on me, I stood up as straight as I could. "Father did not threaten me in any way," I said. "He is an honourable man."

Lord Cochrane nodded to Snodgrass as Mr Todd looked away in evident dismay. I knew then that my honesty had not helped me.

Snodgrass gave his closing argument with some skill and a great deal of personal animosity. Or at least it felt personal when I stood in the dock, and he dedicated his words to ensuring my life became highly unpleasant or very short. Snodgrass cast doubts on my friendship with Mr Gillespie by mentioning that nobody had ever seen us together and reminded the jury that Gillespie's intended doubted that he would befriend me. When he added my involvement in whisky smuggling, I saw the members of the jury nodding. I knew then which way the verdict would be.

Mr Todd tried his best. He reminded the jury that nobody had seen me take the teapot, and all the evidence was either hearsay or circumstantial. They listened, looked at me in my jail-stained clothes, remembered the respectable witnesses who had spoken against me and made up their minds.

After less than ten minutes, the jury returned their verdict.

Lord Cochrane stared at me. "Fiona Gunn," he said. "You have been found guilty of the theft of a silver teapot valued at two guineas. For that, I sentence you to be transported across the seas for a period of seven years." He banged his hammer down. "Take her away."

18

Seven years transportation.
That meant that the government would pack me with hundreds of other convicts and send me to Van Diemen's Land or some other part of Australia to work as a slave in vile conditions. I was in shock as two hefty men escorted me away from that courtroom and down to the same cell as I had inhabited before the trial. It was empty now, with my prostitute companions having gone to wherever the court sent erring women, and the murdering mother sentenced to the gallows.

Strangely, I did not think of their predicament. I only thought of myself and the horror stories that I had heard about Van Diemen's Land. It lay thousands of miles away on the other side of the world, a place of slavery and death, of terrible heat and worse people. I would be mingling with the most depraved sort of individuals, with killers and rapists, real thieves and bigamists.

That was not the worst, though. I would be away from my home, away from my glen, and my family.

That realisation hit me hardest as I slumped in that lonely cell. Nothing in the hills scared me. In my own heather, I could face the foulest weather, frost that slapped you in the face, blinding snow, horizontal rain or the near-perpetual wind. In this dark cell in the midst of the town, I was scared. I did not belong here. I wept for this cruel fate that chance had brought me. I wanted to go home.

"You have a visitor," the female turnkey told me.

I looked up through my tears to see my mother.

"Mother." I was sobbing as she enfolded me in her arms. "Where have you been?"

"They would not let me come," Mother said. "That Campbell held us prisoner until after the trial."

"Is Father with you?"

Mother shook her head. "No, Fiona. Father is away on some business of his own. He sends his love."

"Oh." I desperately wished that Father was there. I wanted his strength and cheerfulness and the solid reassurance of his presence. Although I tried to hide my disappointment, I could not hide my hurt.

"He hasn't forgotten you, Fiona." Mother had not released me. "I promise you that he has not forgotten you."

It was then that I broke down completely. My flow of tears became a waterfall, and I held my mother as though she was my saviour, as she was, of course. That was the first and only time that I ever saw my mother cry as we stood in that dark cell in Perth, with the turnkey at the door, watching and saying nothing.

"They're going to transport me," I said at length when I had spent the worst of my tears.

"I know," Mother said.

"I thought you had all left me alone. I thought you had forgotten all about me." I was sobbing as I spoke.

"We will never forget you. However long you are away, we will be there when you come home." Mother's voice broke as she held me.

"Seven years," I said.

"Seven years, seventy years or seven hundred years, Glen nan

Gall will be your home, and your children's home and your grandchildren's grandchildren's home." Mother spoke fiercely. "Whoever thinks they own it and whatever they do to it, our glen is in our blood, and we belong there like no others will ever do."

"I want to go home," I said.

"I know," Mother held me closer. She lowered her voice to a whisper. "Don't give up hope, Fiona. Never give up hope."

"Does Niall know?" I grasped at another straw, wondering if Niall could break me out of this jail and we could run north and live like Rob Roy in the heather hills.

Mother nodded. "Niall knows," she said slowly.

"Is he coming to see me?" I asked.

"Niall and Catriona MacRae are engaged to be married now," Mother said.

I felt as if somebody had kicked me in the stomach.

"Oh," I said. I could not say anything else for quite some time. I remembered how Niall had looked at Catriona that day we had taunted the militia. That time seemed so long ago and so innocent, yet I suspected that it had finally persuaded Malcolm Campbell to end the distilling in our glen. "I hope they are happy together."

I thought of Niall and Catriona setting up home while I sailed across the world. If I ever found a way to return to Scotland, they would have been married for seven years and more, they would have children while I would be a scarred spinster, unwanted by anybody.

"Oh, God help me." I began to cry again.

"Enough of that, " Mother said sternly. "You are a Gunn, not some soft Low Country girl. You are strong and agile, and intelligent. You can cope with whatever happens, wherever it happens. Now get a hold of yourself."

"Time is up," the turnkey said. "You will have to leave now, Mrs Gunn."

"No, please..." I held out my hand. "Please don't go, Mother."

"I have to." Mother took a step backwards, still with one hand on my shoulder. "Remember what I said. Don't give up hope."

I was staring into her eyes as the turnkey slammed me inside, alone again.

I stared at the closed cell door, feeling sick, yet with Mother's words echoing through my head.

"Don't give up hope."

What did that mean? There was no hope. The judge had handed down his sentence and had condemned me to seven years transportation. What hope could there be? Why had Father not come to see me?

The coach came only two days later. It was a hired chaise with a wiry, unsmiling driver and burly guard with a tall hat, a blunderbuss, and a pair of pistols at his belt. He stared at me, unblinking, as Horne, the Sheriff Officer, escorted me from my cell and down the turnpike stairs to the street outside.

There were three other criminals condemned to transportation, and a crowd gathered to see us depart. Some stared, a few jeered, and one drunken man cheered and tried to encourage the rest to rush in and rescue us. The guard from the coach dismounted at once and tapped him on the head with a short cudgel.

"That's enough from you, my man," he said.

My faint flicker of hope died stillborn.

"Give me your left hand," Horne ordered, and within seconds I was handcuffed to a criminal on both sides and crammed into the coach. I searched the crowd, desperate to see a friendly face, hoping to see Father or Mother.

They were not there.

"Wait!" the Sheriff Officer snarled as the guard hefted his blunderbuss. I flinched as the flared barrel pointed directly at me. I had heard of such weapons and knew that one squeeze of the trigger could spread shot across all four of us prisoners.

Opening the boot of the coach, the Sheriff Officer produced

even heavier shackles, which he fastened around our ankles, so walking was only possible with short steps and great effort. The Officer had hobbled me more effectively than any horse.

"Inside." Horne ordered, shoving me in the back. We clambered inside the coach, having to crawl and struggle because of our chains. We took our seats with a mixture of curses and gasps as the shackles bit into wrists and ankles.

I looked around. I was alone with three criminals inside a prison coach.

Horne banged shut the door.

"Where are we going?" I asked.

The man on my left laughed. "Hell," he said and rattled the chains that connected us. "How long did you get?"

"Seven years," I said.

"What for?"

"They said I was a thief," I told him.

"Are you?" He had a hard, quick accent and with a start, I recognised him as one of the men from the Peter Wallace gang. He was John Hay, the man who had stared at me that exciting night in Forfarshire.

"That's my business," I said. Already I knew that such a man would prey on an innocent from the Highland glens. I had to adapt to this new life quickly.

"I'm John Hay, and I got ten years," he said. "I did assault with intent." He sounded proud of his exploits and his sentence.

"Seven for me," the woman on my right said. "Housebreaking and robbery."

I leaned back and closed my eyes, trying to digest this intelligence. These were the kind of people with whom I was destined to spend the next seven years of my life.

"Hey!" the man opposite kicked me in the shin. "I wouldnae try to sleep here. You dinnae ken what might happen to you!"

"I know you," John Hay stared at me in belated recognition. "Where have I seen you before?"

I said nothing.

"Got it," he said. "You were with the whisky smugglers." He leaned closer to me. "I'll have my fun with you later, my little mountain lassie, my wee peatreekie."

I think it was only then that the full horror of my situation came to me. I stared at my companions, wondering what depths they would sink to and how I could survive seven years in such company.

The Sheriff Officer opened the door again and had a last look at us.

"If any of you give me any trouble," he said, "I'll be in here, and you'll wish you were on the gallows by the time I've done with you." He was a middle-aged, sullen man with neatly shaped side whiskers and the hardest eyes I had ever seen. He nodded twice and slammed shut the door before vaulting onto the coach roof. I heard his heels drumming, and the coach jerked into motion.

"Oh, God," I said.

"We're off to Dundee," John Hay said. "We're off to Sunny Dunny by the sea, eh. I just came from there to be tried. Now, I'm going back to be transported." His laugh was disturbingly high-pitched.

It is a little over twenty miles from Perth to Dundee, the first leg of my journey to the other side of the world. I sat in misery, trying to ignore my companions, and gasping as every jolt of the coach jerked the shackles around my wrists and ankles. Long before we reached Dundee, I was raw and bleeding, as well as out of temper.

"It's lucky they only use light handcuffs here," John said. "Once we're on board, they'll use the twenty-pound weights."

"On board?" I was still confused about what was going to happen.

"Don't you know?" John sneered. "The coach will take us to Dundee docks and then straight onto a smack for London."

"Won't we have any time in Dundee?" I tried to keep the

dismay out of my voice. I had hoped desperately to see Mother or Father one more time.

"None," John Hay said. "They'll time our arrival to meet the tide, so we'll board the smack just before she sails. This time tomorrow, we'll be half-way to London, then, if we're lucky, straight onto a transport ship to Van Diemen's Land. In six or seven months, we'll be there, and our time begins."

I could not resist my shudder. "What if we're unlucky?"

"The hulks," John said. "Caged for weeks or months in an iron cage in a rotting ship, with fever and rats. You and I will be together, though Peatreekie."

The rest of that journey passed in silence except for the occasional gasp as the shackles bit into tender flesh. After another hour, the coach slowed, and I heard the growl of many passing wheels and the clopping of horses' hooves.

"Dundee," John said. "Can you smell it?"

I could. It was a combination of crowded people, ten thousand horses, and human waste. I realised then how much I missed the clean, heather-scented air of my home.

With the windows sealed, I could see nothing of Dundee. I could see nothing except the gaunt, predatory faces of my companions, sunk in vice and wickedness, or perhaps merely unfortunate victims of society's failings. I did not know.

The coach halted briefly. I heard the Sheriff Officer talking to somebody, and then we were moving again.

"We've entered the docks." John winked at me. "Say farewell to old Scotia."

"You're very cheerful," my female companion said, adding a few colourful epithets that fouled the air.

John shrugged. "Old Scotia never done nothing for me," he said. "Australia cannae be any worse, and I've got plans." He grinned at me. "You're part of them, Peatreekie."

Glowering, I tried to kick him and succeeded only in jerking our ankle chain and upsetting my fellow sufferers.

The coach pulled to a halt then rocked as Horne jumped from the roof. He opened the door and peered in.

"Out!"

It was hard to climb out of the coach with both wrists and ankles shackled to other people. I stumbled twice, righted myself and found myself staring into the eyes of John Hay. His smile was pure evil.

"There is nowhere to escape on a ship, Peatreek."

At that moment, I knew that if he tried to take advantage of me, I would kill him. Better be hanged for murder than live under the thumb of a man like him. I held his eyes with all my fear sliding away.

"You can try it," I said, as my Father's blood surged within me.

We were at the side of a dock, with three ships moored alongside and one floating further out. The closest was a two-masted thing with the name *Lochee* painted in white on her black stern and a host of seamen busy on her deck. With Mother's words in my head, I looked around, still hoping for help, but seeing only the merciless face of the Sheriff Officer and the nutmeg-brown guard and driver.

A bevy of seamen crowded off *Lochee*. They looked at us in some curiosity as a broad-shouldered man approached the Sheriff Officer.

"Is this the cargo?"

"Four convicts for the hulks, Captain Wardlaw." Horne produced a file of papers. "Sign here to accept delivery."

Captain Wardlaw looked us over. "I can't be responsible for any losses caused by the weather or any disease they may already have."

"That is understood."

Captain Wardlaw signed for us.

"Get them on board," he said. "Put them abaft the mainmast on deck. I'll not have them fouling up my ship, and they'll be safe enough there." He wrinkled his nose. "If the jail stink gets too much, we'll hose them down right and dandy."

"This way, folks," A tousle-headed seaman held out a hand to help us. "All aboard for the trip, fresh sea air, a healthy breeze, and a quick passage." He eased me onto the deck. "Careful now, my girl."

"Thank you," I said, grateful for any show of kindness.

He looked at me. "That's a Highland accent," he said and changed to Gaelic. "What have you done to get to this state?"

I could have cried to hear my native tongue in this strange place. "I am falsely accused of theft," I said.

"Life can be hard when it goes wrong," he said, still speaking in Gaelic. "I am Kenneth Mackenzie from the Island of Lewis."

"I am Fiona Gunn from Glen nan Gall," I said, desperate for any sign of friendship.

"Stop that heathenish gibbering!" Captain Wardlaw roared. "Get the cargo in irons and get on with your work, Mackenzie."

"I am sorry," Kenneth Mackenzie said. "I must do this." He took us to an area behind the main mast where a long iron bar stretched along the deck. "Sit here," he ordered, and he crouched down while he locked our ankle shackles to the bar.

"What happens if the ship goes down?" Hay asked.

"I'll release you," Mackenzie said.

I had never been on a ship before. The thought of being chained on deck in a storm was so terrifying that I could have fainted. Instead, I concentrated on my surroundings, repeating Mother's words, "don't give up hope," again and again, as if they were a talisman against ill-fortune.

"The tide is with us," Mackenzie muttered. "We'll be underway soon." He scampered off on some nautical mission as Captain Wardlaw roared a string of incomprehensible orders. Sailors unfastened the ropes that tied *Lochee* to the quay, and a busy steam-powered tug pulled us away from the land.

"Don't give up hope," I repeated desperately, "don't give up hope."

The tug hauled us out of the dock and into the tidal glitter of the Firth of Tay. Immediately we hit the firth, the swell rocked the ship up and down in a manner most unsettling to my stomach.

"Cast off the tow rope!" Captain Wardlaw roared, and the line connecting us to the tug dropped into the water. Men on the tug coiled it up, and the little vessel chuffed away back to the docks for its next task.

I watched the spires and towers of Dundee slide away, and then the green hill that dominated the town vanished as our great white sails dropped from the yards, and we were underway. We left the Tay behind and swooped into the North Sea, where waves broke against the hull of the ship, spattering us poor convicts with spray and cold water.

"Don't give up hope," I repeated. "Don't give up hope."

I tried to sleep, squeezing my eyes tight shut in the idea that when I awoke, things would be different, but I could not sleep, and when I opened my eyes, Hay was watching me with an evil grin on his face.

"Sometime soon," Hay said, "I will get my opportunity, Peatreekie, sometime soon."

I stared at him, with something of my old spirit returning. "If you put a finger on me," I said, "I will kill you."

He laughed. I did not stop staring at him, keeping my eyes intent as I poured out all my hatred on my fellow convict. I was already a victim of the spleen of Campbell and Snodgrass. I refused to become a victim of this creature.

From our position on deck, I could see the coast of Scotland slipping away to the right, with the grey-green fields, the friendly blue hills, and the occasional huddle of a coastal village. I watched hungrily, wondering when I would see my homeland again.

There were other boats in the water, mostly small sailing craft busy on their own affairs, with the very occasional steam-powered vessel huffing along in front of a sooty trail of smoke.

"Look." Hay kicked me, setting the chains to rattle. "Say goodbye to Scotland."

I held his gaze until he looked away and repeated my mother's words. "Don't give up hope. Don't give up hope."

"What's that damned fool doing!" I heard Captain Wardlaw say. "He's on a collision course! Blasted steam kettles!"

I looked up. We were heading south about a mile from the coast, with the sails bulging and the ship making all sorts of hideous creaking and groaning noises. I had never been on a ship before. It was noisy and bustling, with the wind howling through the rigging like a demented banshee and the timbers always moving and complaining. If I had not been so numbed by my situation, I would have been terrified on that ship.

The captain was right. One of these new steam vessels was heading straight for us, with its bows breaking the sea, so spray and spindrift rose high and its tall smokestack spewing black fumes. It was an ugly thing to disfigure God's blue ocean, and as soon as I saw it, I felt disquiet.

"Steer to port," Captain Wardlaw ordered and lifted a speaking trumpet from its bracket on the mizzen mast. Putting it to his lips, he roared a mouthful of nearly incomprehensible words, most of which were too ripe for innocent ears, and in a manner that should have blistered the paint on the approaching vessel.

"They're going to ram us," Hay said and again gave that high-pitched laugh. "We'll cheat the Demons yet, boys. We'll drown here rather than serve as slaves for the government!"

"Oh God in heaven!" I prayed in Gaelic, looking around for Kenneth Mackenzie, hoping that he would come and set me free. I did not want to drown here, so far from Glen nan Gall and without ever seeing Father and Mother again.

Somebody stood in the bow of the approaching steamboat. I watched and prayed as the boat altered course towards us, with the water churning creamy-white around its twin side paddles and the wind blowing its smoke this way and that. One minute the smoke was behind the boat, the next, it covered the bodywork, so the dirty black cloud hid the people on board.

"Ahoy, *Lochee*! Ahoy *Lochee*!" The speaking trumpet distorted the voice, so it had a metallic, alien ring. The man in the bows of the steamboat was tall and half-hidden in the smudging smoke.

"Stand clear, mister!" Captain Wardlaw replied. "We've got a timetable to keep, and we're not stopping for anybody, let alone a blasted steam kettle."

"*Lochee*! I have urgent business with your master!"

"You'll have urgent business with Davy Jones unless you stand clear, mister. I'll sink your little boat unless you keep out of my way!" Wardlaw roared out another order that made the seamen scurry around, and more canvas appear from the spars.

Lochee heeled over under the pressure of wind, and the steamboat had to turn away with the water frothing under her paddles.

Not really concerned, I watched listlessly until a gust of wind blew the smoke astern of the steamboat, and I had a clear view of the man in the bows. For an instant, I stared straight into the face of Mr Gillespie, and then *Lochee* surged ahead, and I could see no more.

"Oh, dear God in heaven," I said. "Has he come for me? Or is this some terrible coincidence to increase my hurt?" It was then that the idea came to me. It did not matter why Mr Gillespie was here, it only mattered that he was. Mr Gillespie was the only man who could clear me of the charge of theft by simply stating that he had given me the silver teapot.

With the wind nearly directly astern, *Lochee* was pulling further away from the steamboat. I rattled my chains and shouted to attract attention, but without success. The seamen were far too busy working the ship to pay any heed to a convicted criminal.

"Halloa!" I shouted in English and then in Gaelic, desperate to get somebody to talk to me. I watched as the smoke of the steamboat faded away, and *Lochee* surged southward.

"With this wind," Hay said, "we'll be in London in no time." He pushed his foot against mine. "Then it's hey-ho for the hulks, Peatreek." He laughed again.

I thought of Mr Gillespie on that steamboat and felt the black waves of despair wash over me. If only I had two minutes with him. That would be sufficient time to convince him that I was innocent. I looked behind, hoping to see the smoke. There was none. What was worse, the wind strengthened, so waves broke over the bow, and cold green water surged on board, soaking us as we lay helpless behind the mast.

"Maybe they'll set us free," my female companion said.

Hay laughed again. I became sure that he was insane. "They'll let us drown first," he said. "We don't matter."

Captain Wardlaw had never left the deck. He eyed the straining canvas and snapped orders that saw men roll up the mainsail, so we had only topsails on. *Lochee*'s plunging and rearing eased considerably as our speed dropped.

"That's bad," Hay said. "The slower we sail, the more time we will be chained on deck. At least in the hulks, we're inside, warm and dry."

The weather continued to deteriorate, so Captain Wardlaw, cursing foully, ordered the topsails furled. *Lochee* bucked like a mad horse, and Wardlaw swore again and banged his right fist into his left hand.

"We're moving backwards now," the woman at my side said. "We'll be sinking soon." I heard the panic in her voice. She rattled her chains. "Help!"

The other convicts joined her, yelling and shouting until a seaman walked across to us.

"We're sinking!" The woman said. "Set us free, for God's sake."

"We're not sinking." The man kicked her in the side. "Shut your mouth, or the captain will gag you."

I sat in sodden misery as *Lochee* wallowed and rocked, seemingly at the mercy of the wind. The captain stood at the stern, giving terse orders that saw another scrap of canvas hauled aloft and then we eased closer to the land in the shelter of a bay between two high headlands and with a small village cowering beneath a cliff. The wind moderated at once, and the captain ordered the anchor out, I lay back, gasping with relief and wondering what would happen next.

The crew was busy aloft, repairing minor damage, and then Hay kicked me again.

"We're being watched."

A horseman stood on the southernmost headland, staring at us through a spyglass. I looked away, already satiated with being the object of public curiosity. With the ship's motion now less violent, I felt sudden weariness and closed my eyes, despite my sodden clothes and the discomfort of shackles on my wrists and ankles.

I woke with a start, unaware of where I was and what was happening. I looked around in dismay as the memories returned. There was confusion on deck as the sailors scurried to one side of the ship.

"What's happening?" I asked.

"Some fool's put out from shore," the woman on my right said. "He probably wants to gawp at the convicts, or sell us religious tracts, or condemn us to Hell for our sins."

I closed my eyes again, lost in a mixture of misery and weariness.

"*Lochee* ahoy!" a man's voice called.

"Mr Gillespie?" I looked up. "Was that Mr Gillespie?"

"Who is that fool?" Hay kicked at me again. "Do you know him?"

An open fishing boat thumped against the side of *Lochee*, and three men scrambled aboard. One was Father, stomping right across to me. The second was Sheriff Officer Horne, who had accompanied us from Perth to Dundee, and the third was Mr Gillespie.

"Who the hell are you?" Captain Wardlaw asked.

"You are carrying an innocent woman as a prisoner," Father said, shoving Wardlaw aside. "Where's my daughter?"

"Father?" I shouted. "I'm here!"

"Not for bloody long, you're not!" Father was at my side. "Open these shackles, Captain, or I'll open your skull!"

"Miss Gunn!" Mr Gillespie knelt at my side. "My dear, dear Miss Gunn! If only I had known! What a terrible thing to happen."

"Can you tell them that I'm innocent?" I could not help the tears that welled in my eyes.

"I have already done so," Mr Gillespie said. "And here is the Sheriff Officer with your pardon. You are free, Miss Gunn, and proven innocent."

"Oh, dear God," I said and then wept in his arms.

19

We gathered in Father's cottage. All the Gunns were there, of course, and Niall with Catriona, hand-in-hand and looking as happy as they should be. Mr Gillespie sat at the table with us as I learned what had happened while I had been incarcerated in the jail.

"I was in London on business." Mr Gillespie was quite at ease in our humble cottage. "And I knew nothing about your situation until your father found me."

I reached across and squeezed Father's hand. I should have known he would know what to do.

"Naturally, I dropped everything and came back to Scotland," Mr Gillespie shook his head. "We arrived too late. You were already tried and sentenced. Your father and I tried to stop *Lochee* from sailing, but we could not."

"I saw you," I said.

"And then the wind was too strong for our little steamboat, and we had to return to shore before the sea swamped us."

I nodded. "I was not at my happiest at that point," I said.

"We hired horses from Dundee and followed *Lochee* down the coast, hoping for a miracle, and the good Lord provided one with that nasty squall. *Lochee* put into shelter, and we rode down to the village of St. Abbs and hired a boat. You know the rest."

I nodded, unable to speak after the nightmare of the past few weeks. "Mr Gillespie," I said. "What are your plans for the glen? I heard that you intend to put the illegal distillers out of business."

"That is correct," Mr Gillespie said. "The days of illicit distilling are dying now. Oh, there will always be the odd smuggler with a small still here and there, but the old days of long convoys are gone. You have seen the best of them, Mr Gunn."

"Oh?" Father winked at me. He had other ideas. I hid my smile, just thankful to be home in our warm, crowded, friendly cottage.

"That is why I was in London," Mr Gillespie said. "I was finding out about the new distilling laws. You see, I plan to build a legal distillery in Glen nan Gall."

"Is that so?" Father asked. I could nearly read his mind as he thought of incomers working in his glen.

"It is so," Mr Gillespie said. "I will need a distillery manager to ensure the whisky is of the right quality and men to work the stills and carry the produce." Cunningly, he faced Mother when he asked the next question. "Do you know of any local man who could manage a distillery, Mrs Gunn?"

"I know of one man who is getting a little old to be running around the countryside dodging gaugers and dragoons, and having my daughter in jail is enough for me." Mother patted Father's arm. "I'll talk him round, never you fear."

Mr Gillespie smiled. "Nobody asked who I am or why I chose to buy this glen," he said. "I am astonished at that."

"*Och*, I knew your mother and your father," Mother said. "Your father was James Gillespie. He joined the army at the White Lady's insistence and never came back. I recognised his face in you the first time I saw you."

I was not the only person to stare at Mother.

"You might have said!" I exclaimed.

"Why?" Mother smiled at me. "It was fun finding out what you knew."

"Where have you been all your life?" I was beginning to recover my old spirit.

Mr Gillespie smiled. "I told you the truth, Miss Gunn. My father, James Gillespie, was in the army, as you now know. His regiment was disbanded in British North America, and he remained there. I was brought up in Canada and became a fur trapper."

"Is there so much money in furs?" Father asked.

"We had our own small company," Mr Gillespie said. "We sold out to the Hudson Bay Company of London and made sufficient money to buy the glen." His smile was directed primarily at me. "That was one other reason for my trip to London. The Hudson Bay Company only advanced part of the sale price to me. I had to visit them in person to obtain the balance."

"No wonder you were gone for such a long time," Father said. "Getting money from any company is never easy."

"Now I can afford to get the distillery started," Mr Gillespie said, "and have the House of the Eagle house restored and furnished." He smiled at me again. "Miss Fiona there gave me some ideas how to begin."

I said nothing, remembering Mr Gillespie's later conversation with Charlotte and Amelia when he broadcast my words around.

"I will need help in choosing the correct furniture," Mr Gillespie said.

"I am sure Charlotte Barrow will be adequate for the task." I had not forgotten or forgiven Charlotte's part in putting me in jail.

"Charlotte Barrow?" Mr Gillespie frowned. "Whatever has she got to do with anything?"

"She is your intended," I said, rather more tartly than I

should have, given that Mr Gillespie had freed me from a very bleak future.

"Indeed, she is not." Mr Gillespie said.

"She said she was during my trial," I said. "And you mentioned more than once that you had a lady in mind for a future wife."

"Charlotte Barrow may say what she wishes," Mr Gillespie said. "I have quite another lady in mind for my wife. Indeed, I have had her in mind since the very first day she nearly tumbled into my arms."

I managed a smile. "I must admit to some relief, Mr Gillespie. I have no great love for Miss Charlotte Barrow. However, Amelia Hepburn is not much better."

"Indeed, she is not," Mr Gillespie used the same words. "My intended lady is a patient nurse and can find food where there is none to be had. She cared for me even when it was obvious that my ankle was fit for use. She cleaned up my house and ..." he stopped and looked at me. "I thought of her as Fiona of the Glen."

I must have been staring at him. "Dear God in heaven," I said.

"Mr Gunn," Mr Gillespie spoke formally. "May I have your permission to ask your daughter Fiona for her hand in marriage?"

Father glanced at Mother and then at me. "You may," he said, "but watch for her temper. She can be a fiery woman when she wishes."

"Miss Fiona," Mr Gillespie ignored Father's honest warning. "Will you do me the honour of becoming my wife?"

"We'll need that house completely renovated," I said. "And we need a mattress on that bed. I am not sleeping on the ground."

"Does that mean yes?" Mr Gillespie asked.

I nodded. I could not tell Mr Gillespie that I had loved him from the very first time I saw him, but I had not dared to hope. Now that he had said the words, I allowed my hidden desires and feelings to overtake me, and my smile must have stretched my face from ear to ear. "There is one thing," I said after I had nodded myself silly. "I don't even know your first name."

"Murdoch," he said.

I smiled. "That is a good name."

HISTORICAL NOTE

In the early nineteenth century, illicit whisky distilling and smuggling were rife in the Highlands of Scotland. There was so much that there was virtual warfare between the smugglers and the government. Dragoons and soldiers augmented Excisemen and their riding officers in the contest with the whisky smugglers. The crack of musketry and rattle of cutlasses echoed amidst the lonely hills of the north. There are many tales from these days, with legendary names and deeds, and today there are whisky trails where smugglers once followed their wary paths.

The Highland suffered in the late eighteenth and early nineteenth centuries. Landowners often cleared the glens of people to bring in sheep or to create sporting estates, which made money. Many landlords also raised regiments of soldiers to fight for king and country, with those who refused to join seeing their families evicted. Few of the young men came back home, and those who did frequently found the landowner had emptied their glens when they were fighting tyranny abroad.

At that period, Lowlanders often held Highlanders and any other Celtic person in contempt. Captain Hawley of the 89th Foot thought them: "a detestable race with some excellent exceptions," while in 1847, a Lowland Scottish journalist wrote

HISTORICAL NOTE

the following: "It is a fact that morally and intellectually they are an inferior race to the Lowland Saxon."

Other published books refer to them as 'Donalds' and poked fun at their accents, attitudes, and culture. That attitude is only slowly dying. While I attended a Lowland College of Further Education, a history lecturer proposed that the college should teach Gaelic. The idea was turned down without a single supporting vote. However, since Devolution, there is a slow turnaround of opinion in the country.

Transportation was one way in which 18th and 19th-century justice got rid of their unwanted convicts. Fiona Gunn was unfortunate to be transported for a first offence, as Scottish judges were usually less keen to hand out such a sentence. In Scotland, it was normally more hardened offenders who judges transported, which gave Scottish criminals a bad reputation in Australia. Many of Australia's most notorious bushrangers were from Scotland.

The Peter Wallace Gang also existed. They were a group of about a dozen young desperadoes who haunted Dundee's Scouringburn area in the 1820s. As well as theft, assault, and general mayhem, one of their favourite pastimes was waylaying whisky smugglers and grabbing their stock.

Catriona Gunn
September 2021
Badenoch
Scotland

Dear reader,

We hope you enjoyed reading *Fiona Of The Glen*. Please take a moment to leave a review, even if it's a short one. Your opinion is important to us.

Discover more books by Catriona Gunn at https://www.nextchapter.pub/authors/catriona-gunn

Want to know when one of our books is free or discounted? Join the newsletter at http://eepurl.com/bqqB3H

Best regards,
Catriona Gunn and the Next Chapter Team